Paddy Plays in Dead Mule Swamp

an Anastasia Raven mystery

Joan H. Young

1

"Knick-knack, Paddy- WHACK, give your dog a bone," I sang, thumping the rubber bone on the rug. The large Irish setter named Patrick, nicknamed Paddy, lunged for his toy, but I pulled it out of his reach, and sang the line again, this time thumping the bone on the other side of the overgrown puppy. Paddy wasn't my dog. He belonged to my second cousin, Vic, who was on a trip to Egypt, doing research for the University of Chicago. Since I was the one family member with lots of space, and a house that could stand the dirt, I agreed to keep Paddy for all of July, and part of August.

My name is Anastasia Joy Raven, and I live at the end of East South River Road, at the edge of Dead Mule Swamp. I've been here in Forest County since early spring. Most of my time has been spent trying to revitalize an old house that I bought with money from my divorce settlement. My ex, Roger, and his new friend, Brian, now occupy my former home in the Chicago suburbs, so I moved north and moved on. At least, I'm trying to move on. Some parts of that are going well, renovating the house, for instance.

The building is a basic L-shaped farmstead with a two-story section at right angles to a single-story. I finished the living room project in June, and the result is a large cheerful space. I painted the walls in two shades of blue with white board-and-bead wainscoting and trim, then sanded and varnished the wide pine flooring. The rejuvenated room is clean and inviting. So far, the furnishings consist of a few secondhand pieces from the thrift store, set on a cheap area rug, but I have dreams of a country-comfortable look. When July began, I was still hunting for the right fabric to make curtains, but without close neighbors, having the windows covered didn't matter very much.

I stood up and tucked my light brown pageboy behind my ears, then tried to convince Paddy that his play time was over. He was just over a year old, full of energy, and large. He shed hair like a yak and shook mud balls from the swamp all over the house, including on my new wainscoting. But I couldn't resist his cheerful disposition and deep, love-filled gazes. Paddy-WHACK seemed to be his favorite game, but he'd only been here a few days.

That morning I faced the first real problem that Paddy brought to my life. I didn't know what to do with him when I needed to go out, and I had a commitment to drive out to Hammer Bridge Town and meet Corliss Leonard. I expected to be gone for hours. I didn't think Paddy would tolerate being tied in the yard, and there was no fenced area of any kind on my property. I supposed I'd have to take him with me.

As soon as I opened the front door and stepped onto the porch, the neat and finished look disappeared into apparent disorder. The entire yard was covered with piles—piles of lumber and plywood, a stack of new shingle bundles, a dumpster full of old shingles, gray two-by-fours that could be salvaged, a stack of pre-fab trusses, and a row of new window sashes leaned against a tree covered with plastic sheeting. The porch was littered with tools not currently in use, and walkways made of damaged plywood snaked across the yard between the piles.

This spring I had gotten an itch to add an upstairs screened porch off my bedroom. I wanted to watch the sunlight play over the swamp in the mornings and evenings, and listen to the bird songs and the frog voices. Since the roof was also in bad shape, I decided to roll all my dreams into one huge project. Thus, the mess around my house was impressive. Somehow, my upstairs porch project had grown into a full second story over the living room. I had to borrow some money to do it and put off a kitchen makeover for a while, but the roof couldn't wait.

I wove carefully between saws and containers of supplies. Paddy simply waded through, tipping over a carton of nails on the way. While I was scooping nails back into the box, he began to drag a strip of the plywood walkway across the yard. The dog certainly brought an extra level of chaos to the mess.

I'd continued to employ Gorlowski Construction for projects I couldn't do myself. I'm quite handy, but some work is beyond my abilities. Robert Gorlowski and crew had ripped off my old roof, and the trusses from the single-story. So far, the framing for the new second story had been put in place, and I already liked how much bigger it made the house look. The enclosed porch would provide a cover for the lower slab terrace, and the porch would have access doors from the new large room and from my bedroom. The terrace would also become a more useful outdoor space as a result.

I had to endure a couple of lectures from Robert about why this should have been done before I finished the living room. However, no one who owns a construction business in an underemployed county was going to turn down a chance to do a major overhaul on an old building, knowing that the bank had already approved the loan.

I smiled as I recalled that day. Gilbert Messler, Vice-President of the locally owned State Bank, had beamed as brightly as fresh-minted coins when he escorted me into his paneled office. His philosophy was that newcomers to the county were easy to welcome when they were low-risk and wanted to borrow money. When he heard the particulars of my settlement with Roger, it took less than thirty minutes until papers and a pen were set before me. I signed, and became even more financially committed to the community of Cherry Hill.

Paddy barked as two Gorlowski Construction trucks pulled into the yard, and five men spilled from the doors. One truck was pulling a trailer carrying a large hog hoe. The pup bounded over to them and planted his front feet on Robert's chest.

"Down, Paddy!" I ordered. But the dog ignored me. Robert gently pushed Paddy aside, as he had every morning this week.

He laughed. "Good morning. I think you are going to have to work a little harder on Paddy's training before he gets as big as a pony."

"I know. He's quite a handful, and it's been a long time since I had to deal with a puppy."

Robert's tone became more serious. "We're going to set the trusses today, and it won't be good for him to be running around loose. That's a dangerous enough job as it is. I'd rather not have to watch out for him all the time."

That settled it. "I'll just get his leash and take him with me for the day. I need to find out how he behaves in the car, so we might as well give it a try."

"Sounds good. Take your time. You should really be able to see the shape of your 'new' house by the end of the day."

2

Fortunately, Paddy liked to ride in the car, so he sat quietly on the passenger seat of my navy blue Jeep Cherokee, sniffing the light breeze that blew between the open windows. His leash dangled from his collar where I would be able to grab it easily should the need arise.

This was my first time traveling over to Hammer Bridge Town. I'd been told it wasn't much of a town, but the remnants of a settlement that had sprung up for the construction crew when a bridge had been replaced in the 1980s. I wasn't quite sure what to expect from the town or from the man I was planning to meet. Corliss Leonard was my first assignment.

Not long after Cliff Sorenson's funeral, I had decided to start attending Crossroads Fellowship church. The people seemed genuine and caring, and although I value my independence, I was ready to find a group of people who would be friendly. I hadn't been attending church for quite a few years—Roger really wasn't interested—but so far I was enjoying the upbeat worship times. The church also provided a way for me to be of service to the community, since they sponsored a family help program, called Family Friends.

My friend, Adele Volger, coordinates the program, and she had just assigned Mr. Leonard to me. Corliss had called the church and asked to be enrolled in the adult literacy program. I wasn't yet qualified to be a reading instructor, although I did have some experience teaching at a community college. Instead, I would be the first contact to find out if the church might be able to help in other ways. All I knew so far was that Mr. Leonard was in his mid-fifties and had called requesting a tutor, and he was open to other types of assistance.

Hammer Bridge Town is in the northeast corner of Forest county. Hammer Bridge doesn't span the Petite Sauble River, but rather Hammer Creek, a tributary that flows in from the north and runs deep in the springtime. Most of the land east and north of my property is in the Thousand Lakes State Forest, on both sides of the Petite Sauble River, and includes a lot of Dead Mule Swamp. There aren't many roads that run through the area, and it's wise to choose which side of the river you want to reach before heading into the State Forest because there are only two bridges. One is on Centerline, about three miles west of my house, and the other is far to the east on Kirtland Road, which is also the county line.

"We don't have time to take the long way today, Paddy," I said, patting the dog on the head as we turned off South River Road onto Centerline. "Adele says Centerline north to Sheep Ranch Road, and then straight east is fastest. Do you want to go fast?"

Paddy stuck his long nose out the partially open window and as his ears began to fly in the wind, I swear he grinned. Paddy was fine with fast.

Adele had written on a page from a small notebook, "Just before Hammer Creek look for a blue trailer on the right with Snow White and three Dwarves in the yard." These directions seemed sketchy to me, but she assured me I'd find it easily enough.

Sheep Ranch Road was paved. It looked like the main east-west road north of the State Forest, and in just about twenty minutes the road began a gradual descent which suggested I was approaching Hammer Creek. On the right, splayed up the face of a gentle hill were about thirty old trailers, mostly in a sorry state of repair and widely spaced. I could see the variety of shapes and every single peeling, flaking and fading facade. One main driveway accessed the entire complex, but once the drive crossed the ditch a maze of sand paths wound to the fronts and backs of every trailer. Other than the trailers, the only thing that made this settlement look like a town was a building on the north side of the road that had once been a gas station and convenience store. Grass grew between the cracks of its pavement, several windows had been boarded over, and subsequently the plywood had rotted and broken into a jagged patchwork. Beyond the settlement, the road dipped again, and I assumed the creek was beyond that. The entire tenth-mile sprawl of the "town" was faded, broken-down and immensely sad.

Although I had already been contemplating what had prompted a man in his fifties to decide to learn to read, the desolation of his living situation further piqued my curiosity. But I didn't have to wait long to answer that question. There were several trailers with some blue on them, but only one was painted in a pure garish sky blue with ceramic Disney figures in front. Snow White and her dwarves leaned at precarious angles, just beyond the edge of an unpainted, plywood-enclosed porch attached to the front of the trailer. When I say the blue was "pure," I only mean that it had once been a solid color. The paint was now curling in large flakes like a pine cone opening on a warm day.

I drove into the bare yard and turned off the engine. The porch door opened and two girls arranged themselves on the unpainted steps. The taller girl was clearly a teenager. She came down a step, while the younger girl stayed at the top. This put their faces at about the same level, and I realized they looked very much alike, and were almost certainly sisters. I wondered about their relationship to Corliss Leonard. The girls seemed neither friendly nor hostile, they just stood there, grasping the railing and staring at me. They wore t-shirts with sparkly decoration—one in pink, the other in green—and short cut-off denim shorts. Their young café-au-lait skin was smooth and clear, and their thin limbs were set off attractively by the skimpy clothes. The one difference, other than size, was their hairstyles. The younger girl's hair was braided and beaded into multiple cornrows, while the older girl had a wild, medium-length, cap of loose kinky ringlets.

I suddenly felt insecure. I wondered how it was that one group of people thought they had a right to claim the ability to "help" another group. On the other hand, Corliss Leonard had called requesting a tutor, and invited this visit. I definitely wanted to find out who these girls were and, strangely enough, looked forward to entangling myself even further in the mysteries of life in Forest County.

3

The girls weren't exactly staring at me. They were fixated on Paddy, who was now bow-wowing with excitement and trying to climb out of the four-inch window opening. I pulled him toward me with the leash. I really needed to get more control of this animal. Here I was facing two girls I didn't know, with an irrepressible puppy who was almost as big as the younger child. I opened my door just enough to be able to stand beside the car and still keep Paddy inside.

"Hi, girls," I began. "My name is Ana Raven, and I'm here to see Corliss Leonard. Is he here?"

The older girl answered, "He's our grandpa. He's inside. What kind of dog is that?"

You can count on teens to be concise, at least when responding to an adult. "He's an Irish Setter. He likes to play, but he's just a puppy. He might jump on you if I let him out."

"Let him out, we want to play!" the younger girl suddenly chimed in, clapping her hands.

A man's voice came from the porch, and I assumed it was their grandfather. It carried authority, but did not sound unkind. "Sunny, you come in here and change your clothes first. He might scratch you by accident."

"That's a good idea," I said. "Do you have long pants you could put on? I'd feel bad if he hurt you, even if he didn't mean it. He's really large, and he has to learn to be careful yet. Your name is Sunny?"

"Yes. I'm Sunny and this is Star." She pointed to the older girl, then turned and ran into the trailer.

The teen who had been identified as Star said, "I'll change too, and we can teach the dog some tricks. What's his name?"

"Paddy, it's short for Patrick. Just remember that he's only a puppy, so you need to be firm with him. Don't let him get away with being naughty."

Star flashed a sudden smile, and rolled her eyes toward the direction Sunny had gone. "I know how to do that, no problem," she said.

I laughed and nodded. "You'll do fine, I'm sure. Thanks for being willing to help him burn off some energy."

Star also slipped back into the trailer, and the man whose voice I had heard now appeared at the door of the plywood porch. "I'm Corliss Leonard. We'll just get the girls and the dog acquainted, and then we can visit. I guess you're here from the church?"

"That's right. Is this a good time to talk?"

"Any time's fine by me. My only job is to herd those girls," he said with a chuckle.

He worked his way down the steps somewhat painfully. Here was a man to whom nature had not been kind. One couldn't help but notice his large and round hips, which made him look very much as if an oversized beach ball had been stuffed inside his pants. Judging from the way his suspendered jeans flapped, the heavy hips were supported on skinny legs. His back was bent from the waist at about a forty-five-degree angle; he apparently couldn't straighten up, and he balanced himself with a cane. His arms were skinny too, protruding from the short sleeves of a brown work shirt. His face was long and thin, but he had a full head of straight salt-and-pepper hair and a short grizzled beard. His skin was ruddy and mottled, not an attractive complexion. Forest County is not very diverse, and I couldn't help but wonder if he was the girls' biological grandfather, or if they had been adopted by one of his children.

The girls, now clad in jeans, burst out of the house together and ran toward the car, setting Paddy to barking once again. "Slow down," I admonished, easing the dog out of the car. "Let him get used to you first."

It took some organization, but soon the dog had sniffed the four extended hands and decided the girls were good people. No surprise, I hadn't known him to dislike anyone yet. Within minutes, Star was stroking his silky head, and Sunny was giggling, with her arms around his neck, while Paddy licked her face.

"You take him over the hill to the creek, away from the road," Mr. Leonard said to the girls.

"That sounds great," I added, and handed the leash to Star. I'm 5'5" and she was nearly the same height, but toothpick-like compared to my average forty-something build. The three youngsters sped up the slope and disappeared over the crest of the hill in just a few seconds.

"They'll do fine with your dog. We used to have a Golden, but the poor old thing died last year. The loss was hard on them. It's nice outside, shall we sit out here?"

He motioned me to some mis-matched chairs scattered around a dented patio table sitting in the sand with no patio under it. He walked unevenly in that direction, leaning on the cane. I followed, brushing red dog hair from my pale yellow summer pant suit. I was glad I'd worn cotton; the hairs clung to polyester as if held by an electromagnet. We seated ourselves across from each other. I was thinking we'd had a rather unprofessional beginning.

"Mr. Leonard, I'm not sure I introduced myself to you properly. I'm Anastasia Raven, and I'll be your liaison with the Crossroads Fellowship Family Friends services. People call me Ana."

"I'm pleased to meet you, Anna. I'd appreciate it if you'd call me Len."

"'Ana,' please, as in 'I wanna be your friend.'" I smiled, but I really like people to get my name right. The man held out his hand, and I shook it. His grip wasn't strong, but it wasn't limp either. He seemed physically weak, but genuine. My interest was personal, but it was also official. Most of the assignment for my first meeting was to make observations, and to assess any particular needs.

"What I hope to do today is get acquainted. Do you mind explaining to me about your family?"

"Not at all, ma'am. It's kind of a sad story. I'm glad enough the girls aren't here to have to listen to it all again. Bringing that pup was a real good idea."

"I'm sure Paddy is delighted with the attention," I said, smiling. I didn't admit that bringing the dog was simply expedient, rather than planned.

"Mostly I want to join the literacy program. The short answer to why I want to read, now, is that my wife, the girls' grandma, died this past winter. My Becky was good to me. She never cared that I couldn't read. I used to have a good job driving forklift over at Forest Tech Products, but then I got hurt, and then I had to go on disability. She did our paperwork, and kept track of things. Star tried to take over, but she's not quite old enough to be able to handle it all."

"I'm so sorry about your wife. When did she die?"

"In March. It was cancer. We thought she had it beat, but then it came back and there was nothing anyone could do. It was terrible for Star and Sunny. First they lost their mama, then the dog, and finally their grandma."

"Is their mother dead too?" I asked softly.

"We don't rightly know," Len said, moving his head from side to side and frowning.

4

Len was shaking his head in the negative, but he lifted the tone of the sentence into a beginning, opening a door rather than closing it.

"What do you mean?" I urged, my curiosity aroused.

"Star was eight and Sunny was just a toddler. They lived with Angie, her full name's Angelica—our daughter, and her boyfriend, DuWayne Jefferson. He's the girls' father. Becky and I were worried some. They weren't the best example of a stable family, but they were pretty good parents, and we tried to help out when we could. They lived in the last trailer, that tan and brown one down there." He pointed vaguely to the east.

"I'll never forget that day; it was Monday, June 14, in '04, Angie was out by herself. DuWayne was hauling sand with a friend, and the girls were here with us. Angie—we always called her that, but when she grew up she wanted to use Angelica—she went over to Paula's Place to apply for a job. That's a diner in Waabishki, east of here on the edge of Emily City. It's in Sturgeon county, but that's closer for us than Cherry Hill. Paula said later that there was an interview scheduled with Angie for that morning but she never showed up. Paula didn't think much about it till later; people do that to her all the time—not show up, you know."

I nodded. "Those kinds of jobs have a high turnover rate, that's for sure."

"Angie could've had a better job, but she didn't have much self confidence, and with two little girls she needed something flexible.

"Anyway, we thought she'd been hired and started right away, so didn't worry at all till much later. She often forgot to let us know how long the girls would need to stay here, but we didn't mind. DuWayne came by about nine o'clock that night and picked them up. The next morning, the three of them came back here asking if we'd seen Angie. Of course, we hadn't.

"We called the Sheriff, it was Stan Portman back then, and he said we couldn't even file a missing person's report until she'd been gone twenty-four hours. The next day, she still hadn't come home. I picked up DuWayne and the kids and we all went to the Sheriff's Office, but they kept putting us off.

"We tried to tell him that she wouldn't leave the girls, but folks from this part of the county don't get much respect anyway, and Portman wasn't known for feeling gracious toward people like DuWayne, if you get my drift."

"I do," I said. My stomach was tight. Even though Forest County wasn't very diverse, I hated to hear that outright prejudice still existed.

"Finally, after two days, on Wednesday, the police started making inquiries." I could hear the agitation in the man's voice, and he began to shake from the emotional strain of retelling the story, even seven years after the fact.

"They couldn't find her?"

"Not a trace. DuWayne said she'd felt real peppy, and wanted to walk to Paula's; it's not even three miles. Since it was technically illegal for all four of them to ride in the truck cab, he let her walk. Apparently, no one saw her after she left home that morning. DuWayne dropped the girls off here at about nine. Of course, DuWayne was the prime suspect to have done something to her, but Star insisted that her mother had been there to feed them breakfast and dress Sunny before she left, and then her daddy had put them right in the truck to come here. Even though she was only eight, she told so many details, matched by Sunny, as much as a three-year-old can say, and they kept her in another room so she wasn't copying Star, that there was no way DuWayne would have had time to do anything to Angelica that morning. After he left here, he went to Larry's house, and they hauled sand together all day. Earned $50.00 each, and that was verified too. He just couldn't have fit in anything else."

Len sighed, and he seemed to lean into the table even more than his bent back required.

"Where is DuWayne now?" I asked.

"Gone too." Len sighed again. "He said he couldn't live in a place that treated him so bad, and he went to Chicago. He shows up every few months with a bit of money, and presents for Star and Sunny. But he gave up all rights. We... I, am their full legal guardian. The girls are happy to see their daddy when he comes, but they don't understand why he won't stay."

It was a difficult story to listen to. I could see how poignant it all was to this man whose life had become pretty much a classic tragedy. And yet, he wanted to learn to read, to try to make things better, even yet.

"How do the girls get along at school?" I asked. I was a bit afraid to hear the answer.

"In their work, or how they are treated?"

"Both."

Len brightened and sat up a bit. "Better than you probably think. I have to say that most people in the county don't give a rat's elbow about the color of people's skin. The girls both have friends, but we live so far out here that it's hard for them to get together much. The school bus is their only transportation into town unless I drive them, but that's getting really hard for me to do. Star is itching for her learner's permit, but she can't get into Driver's Ed until this fall."

"Teens are always eager to learn to drive, and I'm sure she can be a big help to you." My comment was obvious, but I wanted Len to know I was interested.

"As for academics, Star is a hard worker and she gets Bs all the time. Sunny is a wonder! Her report cards are full of As and it seems as if she gets them with no effort at all." He hung his head. "I'm the stupid one of the family."

"I hardly think that's true," I said, and I meant it. "You don't talk like someone who isn't intelligent. Do you know any reasons why reading has been difficult for you?"

Len seemed glad to change the subject, even if this topic was only slightly less painful. "Yes, the letters get all mixed up when I look at them. Sometimes a t looks like an f, or a b like a d, and then I get nervous, and they all just swim around like alphabet soup. They call it dyslexia now, but when I was a boy they just called it retarded."

"There are lots of ways to help overcome that," I said.

"Star works so hard at school. I want to show her that I'm willing to study hard too, that good effort can really pay off."

"That's truly admirable," I said, but Len didn't respond. After a few seconds I added, "We don't want to intrude on your life where you don't want us, but are there other ways that Family Friends could help you, in addition to the tutoring?"

"I'd like it a whole lot if there was a woman who would make friends with Star and Sunny. They need someone with a softer touch than an old man, someone who understands girls. At least better than I do. They've got no one to talk to about hair and clothes and female stuff, except for each other. They are good children, but I think they need some female guidance."

5

Barking and shouting from the top of the hill intruded on our conversation. We watched Star throw a stick, and Sunny and Paddy both ran full tilt down the slope in our direction. As they came nearer, my heart sank at what I saw. Paddy was dragging a sodden leash, dripping water and flinging brown globs with every shake of his body, and the girls were well dotted with water spots and mud. Sunny was wet to the knees, her socks sagging over the tops of her sneakers. She was grinning from ear to ear, and so was Paddy. Star was trying to maintain some dignity as the mature one of the group, but her eyes were bright and she broke into a real smile as they came nearer.

"Oh, I'm so sorry," I began, as I stood up. "This dog can't seem to stay out of trouble for ten minutes."

Len laughed, a deep laugh that shook his round hips. "Don't you worry about a little mud. Our trailer isn't one of those fancy starter castles like over in Emily City. I haven't seen those girls so happy for quite a while. You're a real hit here, today."

Sunny ran up to me. I thought she was going to hug me, but Star grabbed her arm, stopping her abruptly. "Don't touch her," Star said in a sharp tone. "You're filthy, and she's wearing good clothes."

Of course, Star had no such luck controlling Paddy, who was trying to rub against my legs while I circled around him in an effort to stay clean.

"Go get one of those old blankets from the back closet," Len said, and Star immediately headed for the house.

"Ana!" said Sunny, quickly glancing at her grandpa, "I mean Ms. Raven; Paddy is the best dog ever. I wish I could play with him again."

"You may call me Ana if it's all right with your grandfather. And I'm sure we could work it out for you to play another time."

"How about 'Miss Ana?'" said Len, turning toward me. "I like the girls to show a little more respect for grownups."

"Miss Ana! Could we?" Sunny caught on quickly.

Before I could answer, Star appeared with a well-worn, but clean, synthetic blanket. She unfolded it, wrapped Paddy expertly from ears to tail and began to rub him down. The dog stood still for her and wagged his tail beneath the blanket, making the Sponge Bob print dance at a furious pace.

"Please," begged Sunny.

"Yes, we can do that," I said to Sunny. To Star, I added, "Thank you. It looks like you've done that before."

"Our Gracie liked to play in the creek, too," Star said. "It's easy enough to wrap him up and hold in the mud." She averted her eyes, and I thought maybe she was trying not to cry.

"Take the blanket with you for now. You can keep your car cleaner that way," said Len.

"I guess I'd better do that. You girls are teaching me a lot about how to take care of a dog. How would you like to come to my house and bake cookies one day soon?"

"That'd be fun," Star said quickly, looking me full in the face for the first time since I'd driven into the yard.

"Hooray!" chimed in her younger sister.

"Is Saturday morning all right?" I asked Len.

He looked at Star and Sunny, "Do you have any other plans?"

They shook their heads. We agreed that I'd pick them up at ten o'clock Saturday, and I bundled Paddy, with the blanket, into the Jeep. Driving out of the dusty driveway, I could see both girls in the rear-view mirror, watching the Jeep and waving. As I turned onto the road, Sunny blew a kiss in my direction.

What had I accomplished? I found out that Len hoped the girls would find a mentor, and he was hoping to be a better example himself. I discovered that because of this exuberant puppy, the mentor might turn out to be me. And I learned that sometimes people who have the least are the most generous. Instead of me leaving anything with the Leonards, I was taking away a blanket and a kiss.

6

It was too early to go home. The construction crew would still be working on the house, so I decided to drive into Emily City and do some shopping. They had a large pet store and I thought there were a couple of places that sold fabric. To get there, I needed to turn right around, go back past the Leonard place and on into the small city. I felt a bit foolish doing this. Would Len think I was returning to spy on them if he saw me go by? Well, I'd just have to take my chances. I turned around in the next driveway and headed east on Sheep Ranch Road.

There was no one outside the blue trailer when I drove past and I hoped I had slipped by unnoticed. I remembered to look for the tan trailer where Angelica and DuWayne had lived, at the edge of Hammer Bridge Town. It was falling apart; some windstorm must have dealt it a deadly blow. Through a hole in the wall I caught a glimpse of a gray table and chairs. I thought it must be hard for the girls to live so close to this reminder of what life with their parents had been like.

As I crossed Hammer Bridge I noted that despite how the road descended some, the bridge was high above the actual creek.

Although it wasn't why I had chosen to come back this way, I recalled what Len had told me about the last day they had seen Angelica. I drove slowly, trying to look at the scenery through the eyes of a young mother who was applying for a job. Beyond the creek, though, there wasn't much to see. Open fields, growing up to scrub oak and pine, abandoned farm houses, and an occasional woodlot didn't inspire me. I liked the country life I was finding in the north, and there was plenty of beauty for those who looked for it, but this particular stretch of road wasn't going to win any awards for most scenic highway.

In about two miles, ranch-style houses began to line both sides of the road, and a sign informed me that I was entering Waabishki. At the next corner, I passed a gas station and then the Suds-Your-Duds Laundromat. Directly opposite was Paula's Place. Apparently the diner was still in business; a number of cars were in the parking lot. I pulled in. After all, it was nearly lunchtime.

Paddy would have to stay in the car, but I found a spot in the shade at the back of the lot. I shook out the blanket and spread it over the seat.

"Hey pup, you need to stay here and be good. Can you do that for me?"

Paddy wagged his tail, his response to most questions.

"I'll bring you a treat."

I locked him in, and tried not to look back as I walked toward the building, but out of the corner of my eye I saw him trying to force his long nose through the small opening I'd left at the top of the window.

The restaurant had been modernized fairly recently. Probably its location on the edge of a larger town helped build the customer base and bring in enough income to cover occasional renovations. There was an entryway with heavy glass doors, and a bulletin board choked with business cards on the wall. Two posters with cars for sale, and another asking for help to locate a lost dog were also taped on the paneling. I wondered if someone had put up pictures of Angelica seven years ago.

When I entered the dining room, I was pleased to find a bright, clean room with both tables and booths, none of which looked damaged or patched with duct tape as they were at the Pine Tree Diner, Cherry Hill's one restaurant. There was plenty of light and every table held a small vase of flowers. A sign said, "Please seat yourself," so I chose a table near the side window where I could keep one eye on my car. It looked as if Paddy had lain down. At least I couldn't see his nose in the window opening. Two blankets and a brush, I thought. I was making a mental list of things dog owners should keep in the car.

I turned my eyes to the restaurant. The flowers weren't real, only silk, but the arrangements were tasteful and cheery. I was glad to see a condiment caddy on each table too. Since I'd had to eat out fairly often this year, I knew how annoying it could be to try to get the attention of a server for ketchup or extra napkins.

After Roger and I had split up, it had taken me a couple of months of searching before I found a place I wanted to live, because Roger had gotten our house. I'd stayed at a motel for a while, before I moved in with Vic's mother, Rita, my mother's cousin. She thought I was having a bad reaction to my divorce, driving around the northwoods, and meeting with realtors to view decrepit old houses. She told me in no uncertain terms that I should get over it and find a good college town, where they needed a Professor of Literature. Perhaps I wasn't being sensible, but it kept my mind off Roger and Brian. I did not want to let my thoughts wander in that direction. Lately I had become more accepting of my situation, but the pain was still there if I opened the door.

And what had drawn me to Cherry Hill and Dead Mule Swamp? I still wasn't really sure. The house I purchased wasn't even particularly attractive. But its location was like something from a half-forgotten childhood dream. The house nestled into a curve of Dead Mule Swamp, the flood plain of the Petite Sauble River, and it was the last building on the maintained road. The area surrounding the yard was solid ground, probably wet in some years, but usually just rich woods. When I had first seen it, in March, there were snowdrops and violets pushing through the snow, and when I signed the papers, pink spring beauty carpeted the ground beneath the trees. I had since found an old trail that wound into the swamp and led to the open water that I could see only from my bedroom window. That was why I wanted the upstairs porch, to see the water better.

"Hello, I'm Madison and I'll be your waitress. What would you like to drink?" the young voice broke through my thoughts.

I smiled at the girl, barely older than Star. "Just water for now, thanks."

"Do you need a menu?" she asked with a cracking of gum.

"Yes," I answered. Something made me add, "Is Paula here today?"

"Yup, she's in the back. I'll see if she can come out. Today's special is ham and cheese on rye with two sides of your choice."

The girl laid a large card encased in plastic in front of me, turned on a heel, and with more annoying gum-cracking, headed for another table.

In a few minutes, she was back, with a glass of water, and order pad in hand. "Have you decided?"

"I'll have the special," I said, "with cottage cheese and a salad. Thousand Island dressing, please."

"American or provolone?"

"Provolone."

"Mustard and mayo?"

"Yes."

"That it?"

"All set for now."

Madison took off on her rounds again, and a woman who was about my age approached the table, carrying two glasses of brown liquid. She wore a bibbed apron over jeans and a t-shirt. Her short salt-and-pepper hair was brushed into a spiky do above a red face. She had a frank and open look and a wide mouth, pulled into a genial smile. She didn't look at all irritated to be called out of the kitchen, and she slid into the other side of the booth.

"Hi I'm Paula Wentworth. I hear you want to talk to me. Have some iced tea on the house." She pushed one of the glasses toward me.

"Thanks. And thanks for talking with me. I'm Ana Raven, from Cherry Hill. I have to confess I'm a bit at a loss for words. I asked if you were here on something of a whim."

Paula laughed. "Works for me. I was ready for a break. It's beastly hot in the kitchen. I don't think I've seen you here before. What's on your mind?"

"I've only lived in the area for a few months and haven't been here before today."

"If I can make a regular customer of you, I'll count it as work and take an extra break later." She grinned. "In reality, the boss never gets to take a break."

I took a sip of the tea. It tasted freshly brewed and refreshing and gave me courage to plow into a topic that was barely my business. "This morning I met the Leonards," I began.

"Ah," said Paula with a knowing look. "The disappearance of Angelica."

"Yes."

"What's your interest?"

While Paula drank tea and fanned her face with the menu card that Madison had left on the table, I explained about the Family Friends program and how I was likely to be seeing a lot more of Star and Sunny. I told her that having more background might help me understand them better.

"Sunny probably doesn't even remember," Paula mused. "I haven't seen them in years. The Leonards don't eat out much. And they sure don't come here. I suppose it's too painful. Star must be in high school by now."

"Corliss said she'll be taking Driver's Ed in the fall."

"Corliss? Oh, you mean Len. Amazing! Well. There was lots of speculation and dirt in the papers, but I only know a little bit about it all, personally. Angelica and I were friends, even though she was younger. She was the same age as my baby brother, Frank. He's close to three-hundred pounds now, but back then he was fit. Played football. Frank and DuWayne were buddies, they both liked football so much, and she would spend time at our house so she could see DuWayne."

"Did her parents object?" I asked.

"Not that he was black, but they didn't like how much time they were spending together. And then she got pregnant. That wasn't part of anybody's plan."

"I was afraid it was something like that."

"She finished school. I'll give her credit. DuWayne was mostly a mooch, but Len got him a job at Forest Tech. DuWayne made enough to buy a trailer in that sorry mess they call Hammer Bridge Town, and they tried to turn it into some kind of home. They did care about each other a lot. It wasn't just a high school crush."

"So DuWayne is the father of both girls?"

"Absolutely! They looked like two peas in a pod in their baby pictures."

"They still look a lot alike." I smiled at Paula, but I could tell she wanted to get on with the story. Madison brought my lunch.

"Would you like something, Miss Wentworth?" she asked

with a bit too much attitude.

"I'm good, Madison. Thanks." Paula turned back to me. "Anyway, DuWayne managed to keep the job for more than a year. That was a bit of a surprise. But then he quit, and they got by on odd jobs and handouts from Len and Becky. Things were pretty tight for a few years. Then there was a big change."

My mouth was full of ham and rye, but I raised my eyebrows in question. Paula took another drink before continuing.

"Suddenly, they had plenty of money. They didn't move into a better place or anything, but they bought a new TV, and a truck, and a lot of other stuff..."

I swallowed. "Oh no! Drugs?"

"I think so. But that wasn't my scene, and Frank was gone in the Army, so I didn't see DuWayne and Angelica much during that time. Then Sunny came along, and things got better and worse."

"What do you mean?"

"She never said so, but my opinion is that Angelica got pregnant in hopes of convincing DuWayne that his family was more important than illegal activities. I don't think they were personally using anything hard, but probably pot and maybe some pills. So, her plan worked. DuWayne must have given up dealing because they quit buying extra things. But after a while any money they had stashed away was obviously gone."

"That seems like a strange way to get someone off drugs."

"I know. It sounds lame, but DuWayne really loved babies. So, that's what I think. They went back to limping along on odd jobs. That's about where they were when Angelica asked me if I needed some help here."

"And you said, 'yes?'"

"I told her to come in and we'd talk. It wasn't going to be a free ride. I interview everyone, even if they're only going to bus tables."

"And that brings us to the day she disappeared?"

"There we are." Paula's gaze roamed over the dining room. "I need to get back to work, but it's been nice to meet you. Stop in again. I'd like to know how those babies are doing."

"Some babies!" I said. "Maybe I'll bring them here for a treat."

"That might work. But you should make sure they feel all

right about coming, first. Star was old enough when it happened to have plenty of memories of her mother."

"I'll keep that in mind," I promised. But I was already talking to Paula's back. She was striding toward a brewing confrontation between a customer and Madison at the cash register.

7

The fuss seemed to be about the price of an item on the man's check, but Paula just smiled and told Madison to ring up the lower charge. I wiped my mouth with the paper napkin and glanced out the window. I'd completely forgotten to keep my eye on the car and the dog, although I had saved him a small bit of sandwich.

Paddy was poking his nose out of the window and scratching at it. His tongue was hanging from one side of his mouth. Suddenly, I felt very guilty at being such an inexperienced dog owner. Without wasting another minute, I headed for the register.

"How was everything?" Madison asked apprehensively.

"Just fine. Could I have some water to go, and maybe some kind of plastic dish? My dog is in the car, and I'm afraid I didn't bring anything for him to drink."

She quickly brought some water in a plastic cup with a styrofoam soup bowl inverted over the top. I paid my tab, and hurried to the car. Gallon jug of water and a dish, I added to my mental list. It only took a minute to unlock the car and Paddy jumped out so fast I couldn't catch his leash. But it was all right, because he was only interested in the water, which he lapped up as fast as I could pour it into the small bowl. I easily picked up the end of the leash, and took him for a short walk under the trees at the back of the parking lot. Plastic bags for dog-doo duty, I mused. I'd need a crate to store all this stuff; it was as bad as having an infant.

I knew from seeing their ads in the *Cherry Hill Herald* that there was a good-sized pet store in Emily City. I decided this was going to be my next stop. Paddy seemed ready to forgive me for letting him get thirsty, since he jumped back in the car with no hesitation. We drove on down the street. Sheep Ranch Road had become 14-Mile Road as soon as we entered Sturgeon County, and then had changed into Main Street at the Waabishki city limit. That seemed to just continue and blend into Emily City with a few box stores and fast food places strung along the way. I easily spotted Fur and Fins on the left and pulled into their spacious parking lot. There was no place in the shade at all. I wondered if the pet store allowed pets, and decided to give it a try.

Paddy was obviously happy to be invited to go with me this time, and we approached the glass doors which slid quietly to the sides. Immediately I was greeted by a cheerful young man.

"Welcome! Bring your dog right in. We always like to meet our customers." He bent to give Paddy a pat on the head. "Sit."

Paddy sat. I was impressed. He didn't always pay attention to me when I gave him commands. The man gave Paddy a small treat.

"His name's Paddy," I offered.

"Shake, Paddy. My name's Brad."

Paddy grinned and thumped his tail on the floor. The young man lifted Paddy's paw and shook it, then gave him another tidbit. After two more tries, Paddy had the game down pat. The man turned to me.

"Since we can't usually get the customers to speak English, even when they are as intelligent as Paddy, I'll have to ask you what he would like today."

I admitted I was nearly clueless about dog care. The truth is we had owned a cockapoo when my son, Chad, was small, but I'd never dealt with a large dog in my life. Chad was now a junior at Michigan Tech, but was spending the summer on Isle Royale.

"Since I'm going to have to take him with me a lot, I need all kinds of things to keep in the car," I said. Paddy, Brad and I walked the aisles and filled a basket. I was intrigued to discover that there were collapsible water bowls made of treated fabric that wouldn't take up a lot of room. A dispenser for plastic bags that fastened on the leash looked very handy. I bought cable and a lead to set up an outside line run. Of course I couldn't resist a couple more toys. Brad suggested ones that would withstand the chewing power of a large dog, and when he cocked his head and held out a book called Training Your Large Puppy, I nodded, and it was added to the basket. Two bags of small training treats went in next, and Brad carried a fifty-pound bag of food to the checkout for me.

While I was pulling out my wallet, I noticed a sign on the counter, "Dog-sitting while you shop - $8 an hour."

"Really?" I asked. Rather a silly question, since they wouldn't post a sign for a service they didn't offer.

"Sure. We have a big grassy area in back, all fenced, with a couple of kennels if we get visitors that don't want to play nicely with each other. It not only helps you, but it's good for socializing the dogs, too."

"Do I need an appointment?"

"Nope. It's strictly a drop-off service. Of course you have to pick the dog up before we close at eight p.m."

"I'd just like time to go to the fabric store."

"We can do that. You need to fill out this form," Brad said, reaching around me beneath the counter. "Abby can help you now. She'll check his tag for a current rabies shot," he added, turning me over to the woman running the cash register.

In a few minutes I had pre-paid for an hour of dog-sitting, and was about $80.00 poorer all together, but feeling much better about doing the other errand I hoped to complete. It was a relief to me that the dog seemed happy to go with almost anyone who would pay attention to him. I stroked Paddy's red head, looked deep into his brown eyes and told him I'd be back soon. His standard answer was a lick and a tail wag, after which he let Brad lead him toward the back door.

I asked for directions to a fabric store, and fortunately Abby knew exactly how to get to one. After my purchases were stowed in the Jeep, I drove away and found the store with no trouble. Most of my hour of freedom was spent wandering between racks of fabric bolts, feeling the material. There were a couple of shades of blue that I liked, and I held them against a barn-red colonial print to see how they would look together. There was some gauzy white material that might look nice with those choices, too. However, I finally realized that I didn't have a good enough idea, yet, to make a decision about the kind of curtains or drapes I wanted. Still, it was fun looking and getting ideas.

I returned for Paddy just before my hour was up. He was as happy to see me as he had been to go with Brad, so apparently I hadn't slipped a notch in his estimation. But it was only three-fifteen. I still needed to kill some time before returning home. It was Thursday, and the construction crew would be working only one more day before the weekend, but I had already heard all the hammering I needed for the week. Also, I wasn't eager to spend the rest of that day inside the house with a large machine swinging its arm around the windows and over my head as it lifted trusses.

"Let's explore the long way home," I said to Paddy, as I opened the front door of the Jeep for him. He jumped in and turned so he could look out the window even before I was able to shut the door.

8

I'd begun keeping a Forest County map in the car. Although many of the county roads are in grids of a mile square, there are quite a few that aren't. Rather than bisecting farms these wandering roads often follow waterways or meander through cool green forests. Also, some roads seem to be through routes, but often they are in non-contiguous segments, with long breaks across swamps or hills where no road has been built. And there are so many rivers and creeks crossing the area that one can never be sure the road you want has a bridge. It was good to be able to check the map. Some of the time it was even correct.

The easy part was to return to Kirtland Road and drive south until I crossed the Petite Sauble River. Then I only had to explore westward until I connected with the roads south of my house, or until I bumped into Centerline. If I got that far west, I could just turn north and go home the familiar way.

"Want to play a game?" I asked Paddy. He didn't say no. "Let's just take the first road west after the river and see where it takes us."

That corner was marked Turtle Dam Road. I was pretty sure I knew where that road led because Turtle Lake is the largest lake in the state forest, and is hard to miss when you even glance at the map. The road was paved and we followed it all the way to where it ended at an expanded turnaround beside the dam, with parking. Several official-looking buildings dotted the neat lawns, and I noted a number of trucks and cars in the parking lot. I saw signs indicating where a foot trail began, and although I wasn't dressed for outdoor activities, I parked, and Paddy began to whine and wiggle.

"Yes, we'll take a short walk," I agreed as I opened the car door.

The dog tugged on his leash and headed toward some people who were clustered near the edge of the parking area. When we reached that spot, I saw it was an overlook above the water. Turtle Lake, with two large islands and several small ones, spread to the northeast. Behind the dam, alongside the lake, was a large grassy lawn with picnic tables, grills, pavilions, a swimming beach and restrooms. A paved trail wound through the area, and I could see camping trailers and tents beyond that. Apparently I'd stumbled onto the main recreation facility.

"This will be a great place to bring Star and Sunny," I told Paddy.

Just then two kayaks, one red and the other a bright yellow, came into view around the corner of an island.

"What fun!" I said. A man next to me turned and looked around to see whom I was addressing. He must have decided he was the one.

"You can rent canoes and kayaks from the north side of the lake," he said. "It would be a lot more convenient if the rentals were here by the camping and picnic areas, but that's the state for you. People like to canoe to the islands."

"Thanks for the information," I answered. "I know some girls who might really enjoy learning to paddle."

"Get 'em while they're young," he added, and walked away.

We stood there a while longer. I watched the kayakers, and Paddy seemed content for a few minutes. When he began to whine I walked him across the dam and found a kiosk with a map showing a large network of foot trails in the forest.

"Not today, Paddy," I said. "You've always got your hiking shoes on, but I sure don't. Let's see if we can find our way home."

Since the dam road was a dead end, I drove back east until I found a road that went to the south. There was no sign on the corner, but the dirt road looked graded and smooth. In a mile I found another unmarked road going west and took that. It ran straight for a mile and turned back to the north. There was no other choice, but it wasn't signed "No Outlet" so I took the corner. It ended abruptly at the river. To my left a track marked "Seasonal - Road Not Plowed in Winter" wound its way along the riverbank. It was smooth dirt, but not as wide as the road I was on. I pulled out the map.

Sure enough, the seasonal road was labeled East South River Road, the same as the road I lived on. But I was pretty certain it didn't connect with my piece. According to the map, however, it did go through to Mulberry Hill Road. That sounded interesting, so I nosed the Jeep past the warning sign and began to bump my way along beside the river. Except for a few large potholes the road wasn't bad at all. Driving slowly was desirable anyway because every so often there was a break in the trees, and the river could be seen shining in the afternoon sun. A dark blue kingfisher swooped low as we passed one of those openings.

The road became narrower and narrower. Soon, branches were occasionally brushing the sides of my vehicle. Paddy seemed to be enjoying the drive, if I could judge by his eagerness to sniff the air and poke his nose out of the window.

"We have a Jeep," I said to him. "We might as well keep going until we can't get through." The truth was, I was enjoying this adventure as much as Paddy. I've always liked knowing my local area, and I hadn't had much time to explore Forest County yet. I hoped Mulberry Hill would be marked because I had forgotten to check the mileage when we turned onto South River Road. There were two-track vehicle paths leading into the woods every so often with no indication as to whether they were roads, driveways, or abandoned logging tracks.

We crept along carefully, but the road didn't get any worse. Finally, we passed an abandoned house on our left. The white paint was mostly gone, the front door was open, and one section of roof on an attached shed was collapsing. The lawn was grown up to weeds and small shrubs. In another tenth of a mile we reached a small turnaround at the river, separated from the water by a guardrail.

"I think we missed our turn," I said. "But let's check this out." I grabbed the map and walked with Paddy to the river's edge. I slipped his leash over my wrist, thinking it wouldn't be a good plan to let him go in the river. Clearly, South River Road used to go through. There were still two concrete bridge abutments in the middle of the river. I was a little confused, because I had already crossed the Petite Sauble River, back on Kirtland Road. So, had the road wandered north again and I hadn't noticed, or where was I?

The map quickly revealed that there was a small river, the Thorpe, coming in from the southwest and flowing into the Petite Sauble. I was only about two miles from my house, and could have driven right home if there were still a bridge. I could see a matching dirt road with a guardrail across the water and realized it had to be the seasonal road that continued beyond my place.

I looked upstream on the Thorpe River, which was wide and straight in this section. The spreading, shallow water rippled over sandbars and around a few large rocks. Much to my amazement there was a bridge less than a half-mile away. With a shake of my head I looked at the map again, and saw that it was a railroad bridge. I'd been told the trains hadn't run for years, but the bridge was still in place. I wondered if it was safe to walk across. There was a bit of a path along the river, but I suspected it had been made by fishermen rather than hikers.

"I think there's a nice walk in your future," I told Paddy. "But let's go home now."

This time I remembered to watch the mileage and easily found Mulberry Hill Road, which did, indeed, go up a steep hill. There were even two switchbacks before I reached the top, where I turned west on Shagbark. After exploring such an assortment of routes, I'd had enough adventuring for one day, and followed the map closely, taking good dirt roads till I reached my house.

The construction crew was gone for the day. Not only were the trusses in place, but they were topped with a plywood roof covered with tarpaper, and a few rows of shingles stairstepped across the black underlayment. It really looked like a new house.

9

The next day was Friday, and I wanted to get things cleaned up before Star and Sunny came on Saturday to bake cookies. The construction crew was also eager to eliminate the piles of building supplies in my yard, since rain was predicted for Sunday. As a result, they worked like maniacs that day, bringing in extra help to finish the shingles on the new roof. The upper floor was sheathed in plywood, and window sashes were fitted to the framing. By the time they left just before dark, the yard was nearly cleared and my new upper floor was somewhat weatherproof.

I hauled the stepladder outside and stretched the cable I'd purchased at the pet store between two trees. I clipped the long lead to it so Paddy could have more freedom outside when I wasn't with him.

My plan was to pick up the girls the next day and take them first to the grocery store. That would allow me to observe them around other people. Although Adele served as the coordinator for the Family Friends program, her primary occupation was proprietor of Volger's Grocery Store, so I called her to see if she would be working Saturday morning. When I told her I'd be shopping with Star and Sunny, she said she'd make it a priority to be in the store. Although she'd seen the girls around, she hadn't actually met them.

Saturday morning, I shut Paddy in his kennel crate. Even though I'd strung the cable run, I hadn't tested its security to leave him for several hours. With a promise of friends to play with soon, I admonished Paddy to be good and headed for Hammer Bridge Town. Star and Sunny were waiting outside at the patio table with Len. Sunny was playing checkers with him

34

while Star fiddled with Sunny's hair. This was the second time I'd seen the girls together, and I realized that Star didn't seem to show any of the typical teenage contempt for younger siblings or authority figures.

When they saw me coming up the driveway, they waved with both arms and ran to meet me. Short shorts and t-shirts seemed to be their usual attire, as that's what they both wore again today.

"Where's Paddy?" asked Sunny with a wail.

"He's home saving up his energy for you," I teased.

"Can I ride in front then?"

"If you get the front seat now, I get it on the way home," Star protested, putting her hands on her skinny hips and sticking out her tongue in mock argument.

I glanced at their grandfather, and he seemed to be enjoying the girls' bantering.

"Good Morning, Len," I said. "What time would you like me to bring them home? Is it OK if they eat lunch with me?"

"Any time this afternoon is fine. We don't have any other plans."

"We packed up some jeans so we can play with Paddy after we bake," Star added, grabbing an overstuffed plastic bag off the table. In seconds the girls were in the car with seat belts buckled and ready to go.

"We'll have a great time." I turned to Len. "We're also going to the store. Is there anything you need?"

"No, but thanks for asking," he said. I wondered if he was just being polite.

Once in the car, Sunny began chatting. She was clearly the more outgoing of the two. As we drove back along Sheep Ranch Road, she explained in a rapid stream of words that she was going into sixth grade in the fall, that she liked math and science best, and hoped Trevor Miller would be in most of her classes.

"Why is that?" I asked.

"He likes to solve math puzzles with me," she said with a toss of her head and no apparent coyness that might indicate she had a crush on Trevor.

When there was a slight break, I glanced back and asked Star what grade she was in.

"I'll be a sophomore," she said. "I turn sixteen in August."

"She likes to read and read and sometimes write poems," Sunny chimed in.

I wondered how much Star liked having her little sister speak for her. I tried to catch Star's eye, but couldn't do it while driving.

"I thought we'd go into town and get some things for lunch," I said.

"Carrots!" said Sunny.

"Strawberries!" added Star at the same time.

"Carrots and strawberries it is then," I said with a laugh.

We parked in the small lot beside Volger's Grocery in Cherry Hill, walked around front and opened the creaking screen door which was shaded by a large maple tree.

"We don't come here much," said Star. "It's closer for us to go to Waabishki to shop. We can even walk there if we have to." I thought of her mother walking to town the last time she was seen but shook off the thoughts of that sad day.

"I'd like you to meet Mrs. Volger," I said, seeing Adele coming out of her office. "She owns this store."

Adele's short gray curls were just loose enough to bounce a bit when she walked, and although she was no longer slim, her appearance was motherly rather than stout. She wore a green apron printed with the store name over black slacks and a polo shirt. Adele likes to know what is happening with everyone, and I was sure she'd been keeping an eye out for us.

"A lady owns the grocery?" Sunny asked. She sounded awed.

"Don't be rude," hissed Star.

After introductions were made, Adele gave each girl a pack of gum and invited them to Youth Group at the church. "We just have games and snacks, and a short devotional," she explained. "It's Sunday evenings at six."

"We don't have any way to get there," Star said. "I don't even get my learner's permit until this fall, and Grandpa can only drive when it's really important. His back hurts too much when he tries to sit up straight."

"We'll try to work something out if you'd like to come," Adele offered.

Sunny looked eager but waited to see what Star had to say. "We'll ask Grandpa," the teenager said. Apparently neither girl was confident of making commitments without permission.

As we shopped, I learned that the girls loved fresh fruits and vegetables. Even though they were poor, their diet of choice wasn't loaded with carbohydrates and sugar. They told me that when their grandmother was alive she had shopped often and fixed healthy meals. They both said they missed that kind of food, as well as cooking with their grandma. We loaded up a cart with produce for a big salad, including strawberries and some other fruits. They agreed they wanted to make chocolate chip cookies. I knew I had the basic ingredients, but we added a large bag of chocolate morsels to the basket.

By the time we reached my house it was nearly noon.

"You built a new house?" asked Sunny as we pulled into the yard.

"It looks like it," I agreed. "But I only added an upstairs to that one section."

"I wish we had that much space," said Star with a sigh. It was the first time I'd heard her say anything that sounded a little envious of having a better life.

As we entered the house, Paddy lifted his head, thumped his tail and opened his mouth in a huge yawn. Both girls ran to his cage.

"You can let him out," I said. "In fact, you had better take him right outside. But come back in quickly. We'll eat lunch first, I think. Are you hungry?"

"Yes," the girls chorused loudly, and raced for the door with Paddy loping behind them.

From the kitchen window I watched them play with the pup. They had forgotten to put on their long pants, but they seemed adept at keeping away from the dog's toenails, dancing around him and teasing him with a stick. Paddy got tired of lunging for a stick he couldn't get, and brought a yellow tennis ball to Sunny. She tossed it to Star. Of course, Paddy raced toward the older girl, who threw the ball to Sunny. The girls seemed completely at ease with the dog. While they played keepaway, I tore up lettuce and washed the other vegetables and fruits we'd bought.

I opened the kitchen door to let in some air, and soon the three playmates tumbled into the kitchen, laughing and shoving each other.

"We can help," Star said, suddenly looking a little bit ashamed.

"OK," I said. "Thanks for giving Paddy some exercise. He needed that." Star looked relieved. She was clearly a little more wary of her relationship with me than Sunny. "There are dishes in that cupboard, and you can pour some drinks. I have lemonade, milk or water; I hope those are all right. I didn't think to get any soda pop. Sunny, the silverware is in that drawer." I pointed to the left of the sink.

"Lemonade is good. I'll have milk later with the cookies," said Sunny, heading for the silverware.

"Wash up first, please," I added.

Within a few minutes we sat down to a lunch of salad, fruits, and some rolls I'd bought earlier in the week. It seemed light, but I knew we'd be filling up with cookies soon. Paddy lay under the table, his nose resting on Sunny's foot.

After eating, we stacked up the dishes and got out the baking utensils. Star measured the shortening, and Sunny scooped up the brown sugar.

"We used to bake with Grandma," began Star.

"We still bake things, but it's not as much fun as it used to be," Sunny finished.

"It's more like work, now that we're doing most of the cooking," Star admitted.

"You have a nice big kitchen. It's fun to do it here," Sunny said as she creamed the moist ingredients together. The girls didn't squabble over who got to do which part of the task at all. Clearly, they had been working as a team for a long time. I looked around at my bargain appliances and old wallpaper. Although I'd bought a stove and refrigerator, I'd postponed the kitchen remodeling in favor of the new upstairs. But seeing it through the eyes of these girls who lived in a small trailer, I realized how grand it really was.

Before long we had rows of warm chocolate chip cookies cooling on a rack, and we'd each swiped more than one finger-full of raw dough. There was lots of giggling involved. I hadn't raised any girls. My only child, Chad, had baked with me when he was small, but cooking with two girls was definitely different from that experience.

"Let's take Paddy outside again before we have cookies. May

we do that, Miss Ana?" asked Sunny.

"Sure," I said. "He'd like that. There's a path over that way, if you'd like to take him for a walk." I pointed in the direction of the trail into the swamp.

"I'm going to change," said Star. "The bugs might be thicker in the woods."

"You can use my bedroom," I said, pointing to the stairs. "There's more room than in the bathroom."

The girls rushed to switch to jeans and then hurried out the door with the dog. They ran down the path into the swamp so quickly I forgot to tell them to take his leash. I wasn't very worried though. He always stayed near me on our walks and that trail only led, eventually, to the seasonal road. There certainly wasn't any dangerous traffic.

As I watched them disappear around the first bend, I contemplated how I might help these girls. Should I ask them how they felt about their mother? Neither of them had brought up the topic yet. Maybe talking about their grandmother's death was a better idea. It was more recent, as was the loss of their dog. They clearly adored Paddy, and must miss—what was her name?—Gracie, very much.

I began to wash up from lunch and baking, and mulled over more possible ways Family Friends might be able to help without seeming to be patronizing. Maybe the church could make sure they had more chances to buy fresh foods. Maybe we could get them a better refrigerator. I hadn't yet been inside their trailer, but it didn't look as if anything was in very good shape, judging from the outside. However, the family obviously had a lot of pride and might not want to accept large gifts.

It was refreshing to see how happy and self-contained Sunny and Star seemed to be, but I was also sure they didn't have many chances to spend time with other kids. I had no idea what their finances were, and I wondered if the girls would have any new clothes to start the next school year.

As I was putting away the dried dishes, my eyes darted to the window when the sounds of yelling drifted through the open door. The dog was running into the yard with something long and white in his mouth. The ends were covered in mud, and so was he. Both girls ran after him, screaming and trying to catch him, but it was Paddy's turn to play keepaway.

"Give that to me," demanded Star. I moved to the door and opened the screen.

Sunny looked at me and yelled, "He's got a big bone!"

10

Paddy trotted up to the stoop and dropped the whitened object at my feet. Star caught up and grabbed the dog's collar.

"Get the hose and wash him down," I said, taking hold of Paddy myself. "Sunny, that old blanket is still on the front porch." I hadn't washed it yet, but that wouldn't matter since it was about to get even dirtier.

Star unwound the hose from where it hung by the kitchen door and began spraying the dog, and I was getting pretty wet myself. Water dripped everywhere; Paddy shook and made it worse, but then Sunny appeared and wrapped the dog in the old blanket. Star began to laugh.

"Come look at your big scary bone," she said to Sunny, between chuckles.

We looked at the thing Paddy had dropped, which had also been washed by all the water flying around. It was, indeed, a long bone, but attached firmly to one end was a deer hoof.

Sunny's bottom lip stuck out and she said with a flounce, "Well, I couldn't tell it was just an old deer leg. There might be dead bodies in that Dead Mule Swamp. Nobody would ever find them. Nobody ever found the dead mule, did they?"

Star put her finger over the open nozzle of the hose to make a fine spray and aimed it at Sunny. The younger girl sputtered and launched herself at Star, causing the teen to sit down hard in what was now a very wet spot in the grass. She dropped the hose, which began to hop around from the water pressure and spray everything in sight. However, the day was hot enough that no one seemed to mind getting wet, and before I succeeded in catching the end of the hose we were all soaked and giggling.

"OK," I said. "We better get cleaned up and eat some cookies. Clip Paddy on his new line over there so he can dry off."

We stripped our wet sneakers and socks, left them outside, and then all went upstairs to change. I loaned the girls some dry t-shirts and they put on their shorts again. The shirts were too big on both of them, but they didn't seem to care. Sunny impulsively gave me a little hug after she slipped into the Michigan Tech shirt I handed her. It hung below her shorts like a dress.

The cookies and cold milk hit the spot after our exercise, and we sat on the lower porch, which I had started calling the terrace, eating them and licking chocolate off our fingers.

"Would you like to go to Youth Group tomorrow or maybe next week?" I asked. "If your grandfather says it's OK, I'll be glad to pick you up and take you home."

"I'd rather come here again," said Sunny without any hesitation.

"Me too," said Star. She sort of ducked her head and then took a deep breath. "I saw you have a sewing machine."

"I do." It was set up in my bedroom, although I had plans to make a nice sewing area in my new room.

"Grandma was teaching me to sew. We had just started a skirt and vest that wasn't too hard. But then she died..."

"Would you like me to help you finish it?" I asked, realizing that my opportunity to do something meaningful had just been handed to me.

"I think it's too small for me now. But maybe I could get a new pattern and material. I have a little money saved up from picking berries for the farm market."

"I like that material," Sunny asserted. "Do you think I could learn how too? Could I have the one that's too small for you?"

"We can do that. How about if we go to the fabric store next Saturday?" I asked them.

Star agreed to let Sunny have her previous fabric, and we made plans to shop the following weekend. I didn't press them about Youth Group.

It was after four o'clock when I returned home from dropping them off at their trailer. I had insisted they take most of the cookies with them, and some of the salad too. It had been a wonderful day, and I was definitely becoming fond of both girls. They were already more than just an assignment to me, but I was exhausted.

The next day, Sunday, the predicted rains came in great white sheets of water making it difficult to see the trees beyond my yard. I skipped church. The old part of the roof, over my bedroom, hadn't been re-shingled yet, and I climbed to the attic every few hours to empty the pan I kept placed under a leak. Paddy and I huddled in the house. We worked on reinforcing the "shake" command and began on "heel" and "stay." In between lessons I read the puppy training book and dozed. Paddy just dozed.

Monday, Robert Gorlowski called to say that he wouldn't be working until things dried out a bit. I told him the old leak was worse than ever, and he said they'd take on that section of roof next, and start the siding on the new upstairs. I wandered around my new room, making plans for a sewing area and maybe a library corner. The area was one large room, and I intended to keep it that way. I did the laundry, including the muddy Sponge Bob blanket.

In the afternoon the sun came out, so Paddy and I took a long walk down the extension of South River Road, farther than I'd gone before.

When the road emerged from the trees of the swamp and ran along the river I began to pay closer attention. Pretty soon we reached what I now knew was the confluence of the Thorpe and the Petite Sauble Rivers. The Thorpe and the road curved around to the southwest, almost ninety degrees different from the southeast direction the road had been going. Just a little farther along, the dirt widened, and I could see where the road used to branch and cross the Thorpe. I was now on the west side of the guardrail I'd spotted from the other bank just a few days previous. The defunct railroad bridge was about a half-mile upstream to the south.

After a day inside, Paddy and I were both ready for some exercise, and we continued down the narrow dirt road toward the bridge. It appeared safe and solid with stout, black and smelly wood timbers. The ties were placed close together, so it wouldn't even be too scary to walk across. I tugged on Paddy's leash and although he whined, he came along. My size sevens easily bridged the gaps between the ties, but he placed his paws carefully. Near midstream, just as he was getting confident, his right front foot slipped through a gap, and Paddy stumbled, his shoulder roughly bumping the edge of the tie. He woofed and scrabbled at the splintery wood, pulling the dangling leg from the space. He looked up at me with raised eyebrows, then down at the swirling water a dozen feet below. Nevertheless, he continued across the bridge without balking. Once we reached the far bank, I could see the trail along the shore that must lead to this end of the road.

"We've found an interesting route," I told Paddy. "But it would be a bit too long to walk to the recreation area. We'd be too tired to recreate!"

Paddy wasn't too eager to re-cross the bridge, but we walked slowly, and he watched his footing. When we returned home, I checked the map. According to the scale, we had hiked about five miles, and that was plenty for both of us.

11

Since meeting Cora Baker in May, I'd been spending some time with her each week, usually on Tuesdays. Cora lives in the southwest corner of the county at the end of Brown Trout Lane. Although her house is a cozy cabin on the Pottawatomi River, the most intriguing thing about Cora's place is that she is privately assembling a Forest County museum in a pole barn on her property. When I met her she had already been working hard to inventory the entire collection in a computer database, but it was way too big a job for one person. I like Cora a lot, and I'd been helping with the project ever since we figured out who murdered Cliff Sorensen, by using information from her newspaper archive. I hoped to find out a lot more about Angelica Leonard from Cora.

So, on Tuesday morning Paddy and I pulled into Cora's yard just as she was stepping out of her kitchen door. She wore clean but faded overalls over a crisp blouse, her signature style. Today the blouse was green, and she had her gray braids pinned around her head, which indicated a get-down-to-business mood. I'd called to warn her that I was bringing the dog. She thought it would be all right for him to stay in the office with us, and in fact, Paddy lay down placidly beside the computer desk when I positioned myself at the keyboard. So far, so good.

We were still working on taking inventory of the boxes we'd brought down from the upstairs storage area over a month before. It took a long time to enter all the information about each item, decide if it would be displayed or stored and then actually take care of it. Cora pulled open the flaps on a cardboard box and lifted a stack of delicate white baby clothes trimmed with handmade lace onto the table beside the computer. As always, there was also a page of lined paper in the box covered with Cora's cramped handwriting. She made careful notes about every item at the time it was collected.

"How's it going with your red friend?" she asked, nodding at Paddy.

"He's certainly brought more activity to my life. He needs to have a decent walk several times a day or he can't lie still."

"I guess that means we won't get much done today," Cora said, but she chuckled, so I knew she wasn't upset.

"We'll see how it goes. But I want to talk to you about something, anyway."

"What's that?"

"I've gotten my first assignment with Family Friends, and they sent me to meet Corliss Leonard and his granddaughters."

"I think I know where this is going."

"Corliss... Len... told me about Angelica's disappearance, and I thought I should at least read the news articles about it. It looks like I'll be spending some time with Star and Sunny. I'd like to understand as much as I can about what happened."

"You're welcome to read the papers, of course, but they won't enlighten you much more than what you probably heard from Len. The whole thing came to a dead end really quickly. There wasn't much of an investigation, to tell you the truth."

"You remember when it happened, then?"

"Sure. The Sheriff questioned that boyfriend of hers..."

"DuWayne."

"Yes, I'd forgotten his name. But, anyway, his whole day was accounted for, and most everyone believed that she just hitched a ride and got away from him."

"Len seemed to think they got along really well." I didn't mention talking with Paula.

"I guess DuWayne was OK. I talked with him a few times in town and he was polite—not arrogant or disrespectful, but he ran around with some pretty rough friends. Mostly, he spent time with Marko Louama's boy, Larry. Larry's been in trouble with the law since he was in junior high. There were a couple of others in that group, too. Some girl from Emily City and another young tough whose name I don't know. But the girl was Mexican, I think. I saw them a lot because I lived in town then." Cora hesitated.

"I know you used to be married to Jerry Caulfield," I admitted.

"Hmmm, I suppose that nosy Adele told you."

I didn't say anything. I'd already learned that Cora's relationship with Jerry, the owner and editor of the *Cherry Hill Herald*, was a very sore topic.

Cora continued, "Well, we lived right there, two blocks from Main Street, behind the newspaper office. I couldn't help but see them. There's an empty lot beside the office, and the building next to that was vacant then, too. That whole group of kids—I guess most of them were done with high school, but they were kids to me—thought that was an out-of-the-way place to hang out. They'd laugh and smoke and push each other around. Sometimes other kids came by."

"Why were they in Cherry Hill if DuWayne and Angelica lived in Hammer Bridge Town, and the other girl was from Emily City?"

"That's a good question, isn't it?" Cora said sarcastically. "I think they were all dealing drugs. There was a lot of reaching into pockets and passing things back and forth while trying to stay in the shadows."

"How could Angelica spend time there? She had two little girls."

"I have to be honest and say that after the younger one was born Angelica hardly ever came around with the gang. Before that, though, she'd just leave the other girl with her parents. They were clueless as to what their daughter was up to."

"Did you ever see DuWayne hit Angelica?"

"One night he slapped her pretty hard, but she slapped him right back. That Larry Louama was the one I didn't trust, though. He had a mean streak a mile wide. Assaulted John Aho at the gas station when he was only sixteen, because the pop machine was out of order. Went after him with a tire iron, but no one was seriously hurt and John didn't press charges. A foolish decision, if you ask me."

"Wow, this doesn't sound like the Angelica I've heard about."

"Parents are always a little blind, don't you think? I'll see if I can remember anything else, but maybe we could work on these baby clothes now." She picked up the sheet of notes from the stack of small garments, and I turned to the database and pulled up a screen for a new item.

Cora and I concentrated on inventory for a couple of hours, after which we walked Paddy the length of Brown Trout Lane. I had remembered to bring some training treats, and we each practiced his new commands with him. The only other fact I learned about Angelica's friends was that Larry Louama had finally been sent to prison for assault about four years previously.

I left Cora's mid-afternoon, and spent the evening raking my yard and admiring my "new" house from all sides. Robert had managed to match the old clapboards with some salvaged siding from a demolition. As soon as it was all painted, the house would almost look as if it had always had two stories throughout. I liked it a lot. Between raking, hauling tubs of debris, and bending to pick up Paddy's tennis ball after each retrieval, I knew I was going to be sore the next day. But Paddy was catching on that he had to drop the ball when I told him "give," if he wanted it to be thrown again.

There was supposed to be a meeting of the Family Friends committee on Thursday. I was looking forward to that, not only so I could report on my progress with the Leonards, but also because John Aho was a committee member. I wanted to hear more about Larry Louama. However, on Wednesday evening Adele called and cancelled the whole thing, saying she had a sore throat. She'd contacted the literacy tutor, and Corliss Leonard would begin meeting with her at the library.

My new upstairs was a mess with plaster dust hanging in the air, but by the end of the week the taping and sanding were done, and Gorlowski's crew was moving on to some other job. I tried to clear the chalky residue from enough surfaces to make a clean work space and to clear my mind from prejudicial thoughts about Angelica's friends.

12

Saturday came, and I had arranged to swing by the trailer in Hammer Bridge Town to get Star and Sunny. They planned to show me the material and pattern that Star already had, and then we'd go into Emily City and visit the fabric store.

Paddy came along for the ride, and I planned to leave him at Fur and Fins for an hour of dog-sitting. I knew the staff would also work on some training with him; I figured a little more schooling couldn't hurt.

When I reached the Leonard trailer, the girls were not waiting outside, so I parked in their sandy yard, told Paddy to be good, and climbed the crooked steps. As soon as I knocked on the door, Star opened it and invited me inside. I was a little surprised at her casual attitude, thinking she might be embarrassed about their low-income living arrangements.

Len was seated on the couch folding a basket of laundry, and Sunny was eating toast with red jelly at the counter which served to divide the kitchen from the living room. It was a typical set-up for a single-wide trailer, made with cheap materials. The dark finish of the cupboard doors was damaged at many corners, revealing inexpensive press board, and the Formica countertop was worn. I remembered to look at the appliances. The stove had chipped enamel, and the refrigerator was rusting. The handle was broken. The refrigerator probably had been purchased used when the settlement had sprung up. Everything looked beat-up and dingy, but the rooms were clean. There were no sagging curtain rods, or gaping holes in the paneling with erupting insulation, so typical of old mobile homes which have been subjected to years of family life. Actually, I was impressed.

"Good morning," Len greeted me.

"Good morning, yourself," I countered. "I hear you're going to let me steal these girls for another day."

He made a noise something between a laugh and a snort. "I don't think I had much to say about it. They've made it pretty clear they intend to annoy you as much as you'll let them."

Sunny licked jelly from her fingers. "We aren't annoying, Grandpa," she said. "Miss Ana likes us, and besides, we already did our chores, so we can go. You said so."

I smiled and shrugged as if to say, "I can't argue with that."

Len said, "I was only teasing, Sunshine. Wash up and show Miss Ana that project your sister was working on with the clothes."

While this exchange was happening I had been looking around the room, thinking I could learn a bit more about the family from their possessions. The thing which immediately caught my eye was a tall set of shelves across the inside wall of the living room. It was filled with hardback books, and I thought it was an amazing thing to find in the small home of a poor man who couldn't read.

"Tell me about your books," I said to Len as I crossed to look at some of the titles.

"Oh, you know, my Becky was a great one for reading. She bought used books at yard sales and would read to all of us in the evenings. We kept the best books, and traded the others for more. When the girls got old enough they would take a turn with the reading, too. It's one of the things I miss the most."

"I still read to us, Grandpa," Star said from the kitchen where she was rinsing off Sunny's plate. She sounded hurt.

"You do, you do," he said. "And I love you for it. I just miss your Grandma. I can't help it."

Star came and put her arms around Len. I didn't want to stare, so I turned to the bookcase. It was filled with classics of all kinds. I saw To Kill a Mockingbird, Little Women, Jane Eyre, and Red Badge of Courage, just for starters. One shelf was filled with Nancy Drew mysteries, the Chronicles of Narnia, Harry Potter books, and other volumes for younger readers. Below that was a row of history and philosophy books. I certainly had found the reason Len didn't sound uneducated.

Len's voice brought me back from my thoughts. "That's

Angie's senior picture." At the end of one row of books was an eight-by-ten photo of a rather plain girl with the same long face as Len, but she had a nice smile. It looked as if she'd had her hair done professionally for the picture as it curled in soft, even waves around her face. Beside that was a framed snapshot of the same young woman with a dark man who was holding the hand of a child. Angie cradled a baby. She looked much older than she had when the school picture was taken, but the difference couldn't have been more than five years. It wasn't a great photo, and it was difficult to discern the features of the man who must be DuWayne.

"See our school pictures!" said Sunny, returning to the living room and pointing to the other wall. Two frames, the kind designed to hold a small print from each school year in an oval around the edge, with the current large photo in the middle, displayed the growth of the two girls. I went over to study them. Every one of Star's pictures showed a serious expression. I tried to figure out which one corresponded to the year Angelica had disappeared. Sunny, on the other hand, seemed to have a disposition to match her name, and she was smiling widely in all her photos, even the one with no front teeth.

"Let's look at the pattern and not waste any more time," Star said.

She had wiped down the counter, and she laid out the garment she had begun a year ago. It was to be a simple straight skirt, paired with a lined vest. She had chosen an African print in turquoise and yellows, overlaid with black geometric designs. Fortunately the pattern was only pinned on the fabric, not yet cut out, so we'd be able to make adjustments for Sunny.

"This will be nice," I agreed. "You really don't mind not choosing something new?" I asked the younger girl.

"I like this material a lot, but could I look in the pattern book for a different kind of skirt?"

"Sure," I answered. "Are we ready to go? Let's take this along." I refolded the fabric and slid it into the bag it had been stored in.

Len held out some folded clothing. "Here are the shirts you loaned the girls."

"Thanks," I said. "Are we ready, then?"

"I get to sit in back with Paddy," Sunny sang out. Clearly, when the dog was around, I had second billing.

"Fine with me; I'll take the front," said Star.

"Hold on," I said, "We have to drop Paddy off at the pet store before we shop. He'll get some exercise there, so we'll be able to work a little bit when we get to my house."

Without too much fuss or delay we delivered Paddy to Fur and Fins, and continued to the fabric shop. Although both girls had been in a store full of bolts of material before, it wasn't something they had done very often, and they were delighted to just walk around looking at pretty fabrics for more than a few minutes. I learned that Sunny liked blues and Star was partial to orange, which seemed odd to me, given her reserved nature, but I knew it was an "in" color. Maybe she had hopes of fitting into her social group more easily.

Star had her own money and she gravitated almost immediately to an expensive, soft, salmon-colored blend with a nice drape. She went in search of a pattern that would work with the fabric. Since she seemed to have a pretty good idea of what she wanted, I focused on Sunny who was flipping through the big pattern book, clearly not knowing what to look for.

I showed her how to find the section with girls' clothes, and then suggested she look at the extra-simple patterns. She pointed to a skirt that was fuller than the one in Star's former pattern, with a sash belt, and asked me if that was OK. I told her, with some relief, that it would be a great choice. I thought the style was more suitable for a pre-teen than the shorter, straighter skirt. I pulled the fabric we had brought along out of the bag, folded it and hand gathered one edge to mimic the lines of the pattern. Sunny stood in front of a mirror and when I held the "skirt" in front of her she squealed her pleasure.

Meanwhile, Star asked me to come look at a pattern. She had selected a tunic with slightly flared sleeves that could be worn over pants, with or without a belt. It would be beautiful in the salmon fabric, and wouldn't be out of style in six months. Star apparently had natural fashion sense. She wanted to know if I thought the front opening would be too hard, and I assured her that we could do the placket together.

Of course, we also had to select thread, interfacing, and a zipper for the skirt.

We made our purchases, picked up the dog, and arrived back at my house just in time to think about lunch. I didn't have hopes of getting much actual sewing done today, but after we ate (salad again, by advance request, and turkey sandwiches) we took the shopping bags upstairs and began to figure out which pattern pieces we would need.

I remembered that Sunny had said she liked puzzles, and as soon as I explained how the pieces were labeled she instantly grasped how they went together. Star seemed to struggle with the concepts a little more, but I pulled a caftan out of my closet to show her, and she saw how the placket front facing would work. We lightly pressed the paper patterns, and then I sent them both outside to play with Paddy for a while. Frankly, I needed a break.

13

Star and Sunny were almost too good to be true. Although I was tired, it was not because the girls were a trial. They were polite, neat, and hard-working. I thought about that as I stacked the smoothed pattern pieces, setting them aside to await our next sewing session. The girls were probably on their best behavior with me. Perhaps their grandfather had warned them to be good, or maybe they were somewhat like newly-adopted orphans—afraid they'd be sent back if they weren't perfect. It made me feel special, but it was also intimidating. I couldn't live up to such a high standard for the long haul. Well, maybe I could pull it off one day a week. But I also knew that a perfect adult wasn't what they needed. And I didn't want to be a mother substitute.

My Chad was almost grown. I was fine with that. My thoughts drifted to Chad's summer pursuit, researching moose on Isle Royale in Lake Superior. I hoped I'd hear from him sometime soon, but they only had intermittent phone service where he was, and I knew that I might not hear anything until he arrived for a scheduled visit in late August. He hadn't yet seen my house in Dead Mule Swamp.

Thinking of mothers, I guessed that Sunny didn't remember much, if anything, about Angelica. But, I wasn't sure why Star had nothing at all to say. Surely she had memories of her mother. She hadn't said a word when Len was pointing out the pictures that morning. Len implied that they still saw their father occasionally. I wondered if I should try to get them to talk about their parents. Then I wondered how to make that happen. Should I just ask? I wasn't sure I was up to the task of helping children with serious trauma in their past.

I crossed through my bedroom and looked out a window on the side of the house facing the swamp. I couldn't see the girls or the dog. They must have taken the trail. I wished they had let me know that they were leaving the yard, but I hadn't told them they should, so I could hardly complain. And hadn't I just been grousing that they seemed too perfect? I glanced at my watch and realized I'd been mulling over the situation for nearly a half hour. What on earth had the girls found to do?

I saw a movement in the trees to my left, on the other corner of the yard from the trail, and Star jogged into the mowed area. She looked a little breathless and flustered. "Miss Ana," she called.

I pushed open the window and answered, "Up here, Star."

"You need to help us get Paddy. He's found something and we can't get him to come back to the house with us. He's acting really weird."

"All right, I'll be right down."

This seemed odd. The dog had stayed close to the girls when he'd been out with them before. I hurried down the stairs and out the kitchen door to meet Star. Just then, Paddy and Sunny burst from the same direction as Star had come. Paddy had a yellow circular object in his mouth. It didn't look right for one of his tennis balls, and in fact, the ball in current use was practically at my feet. Sunny was once again chasing the dog and yelling. It was pretty much the same scene as a week ago, but with less wet mud. And a different prize.

"Come, Paddy," I said in my sternest dog-trainer voice. He actually obeyed and came to me, wagging his tail. "Sit." He sat. I could hardly believe my luck, but I pushed it a little farther, "Give." He dropped the object at my feet, and I picked it up. He looked at me with his liquid brown eyes, and I checked my pocket for treats. I did have one, and rewarded Paddy for his exceptionally good performance.

The yellow thing was a rubbery band about a half-inch wide, and maybe two-and-a-half inches in diameter. It looked like one of those bracelets you could buy to support cancer research or some other cause. It seemed to be scratched or roughed up. I brushed some of the dirt off, and in the process the band rolled so that the inside became the outside and I realized there were words inscribed in the rubber.

I was rubbing my finger across them, to make them readable when Star suddenly snatched the ring out of my hands. "Sunny!" she exclaimed. Her voice was high and angry. "You shouldn't have worn this today. How could you?" I could hear her voice crack, and a glance at her face showed pain as well as anger. I couldn't figure out what was happening.

Sunny's face darkened and her eyes flashed. "I didn't! It's not mine."

Although Sunny was looking stormy, I watched the color drain away from Star's face. Her skin turned a muddy gray-brown, and she began to sink to the ground. I grabbed for her and managed to keep her from toppling over, but she ended up on the grass in a tangle of knees and elbows, clutching the bracelet. Tears were already running down her face.

"Star! What's going on? What's wrong?" I asked. I looked to Sunny for assistance, but she wasn't looking very well either and came over to sit beside her sister.

"Let me see," Sunny whispered, and Star rubbed the dirty band against her cheek, and then handed it to the younger girl who took it reverently.

Star lifted her tear-streaked face to me, sniffed, and said, "It belongs to our mom. Both of ours are home. Put away to keep them safe, you know."

"Surely there are lots of rubber bracelets," I protested. But something in Star's eyes made me stop.

"Not like this one. Our mother special ordered these. You can get custom ones for only a few dollars. Show her what it says, Sunny."

Sunny handed me the band. I turned it and read the inscription: "Sunny and Star - Happy Birthdays – Mommy Angel."

Star explained, "We all have the same birthday. It's so weird. Sunny and I were both born on August 21, but five years apart. And even stranger is that it was Mom's birthday, too. All of us girls were born on the same date. That's why she gave us the names we have. She said we were all heavenly. The three of us always wore these bracelets after she bought them, like a secret club or something. I suppose it was silly, but we were little and it was fun."

I sat down beside Star and put my arms around her. She

leaned against me. She wasn't crying any longer, but every so often a shudder ran through her body. Sunny crept around to the other side of me, and I kept one arm around Star but pulled Sunny close with the other. Paddy laid his chin across Sunny's knees. We sat there quietly for several minutes. Sunny seemed sad and curious, but less broken up than her sister.

"How did Mom's bracelet get in the swamp?" Sunny asked.

"That's an important question," I said. "I think we are going to have to call the police."

14

"Why should we call the police?" asked Sunny.

"You little dumbbell," said Star, giving her sister a withering look. "This means that Mom was here, after that morning. It's the first thing anybody's ever found of hers."

"She wouldn't go for a walk way over here. That doesn't make sense."

"You just don't get it!" Star shook her head. "No, you're too young. She was here with someone, or they brought her here. Don't you see? Mom's dead, and Paddy just found her body."

Sunny said, "Oh," in a flat voice and shrank into a tight little ball beside me.

"Come on, let's go inside," I pulled the girls to their feet. "We don't know that for certain, but we have to report what we do know." However, I was pretty sure Star was right.

Once we were in the house, Star asked if I had any decaf tea and if she could fix some. I knew that giving her something to do would be calming, so I told her where to find my stash of herbal teas, and she and Sunny took over the kitchen.

I decided to call the Sheriff first, and Len second. It seemed important to get things moving. I wanted to call Tracy Jarvi, the young female Chief of Police in Cherry Hill. I got along well with Tracy, especially since she had helped me, more than once. I wanted her support, but I couldn't think of a way that Paddy's find could be part of her official duties since I live outside the village limits, and I didn't feel close enough to just call her as a friend.

I dialed the Forest County Sheriff's Department and was transferred to a Detective Dennis Milford, someone I did not know at all. He sounded bored. It took several minutes to

58

explain how the bracelet we had found would be of interest to the police, but he finally agreed to send a squad car out to my place.

Next I called Corliss Leonard. This conversation was much more difficult for the opposite reason. Len understood immediately how significant the events of the afternoon were. I asked if he would like me to come get him, although I wondered how I could do that, stay with the girls, and be here when the police arrived, all at the same time. But he said he'd drive himself to my place, if I didn't mind. I assured him I'd be glad to have him come, and told him the girls would need his support. A guilty image of Len torturing himself into an upright position in order to drive intruded on my sympathies, but I knew we all needed him to be here. I told him we'd be watching for him.

These calls took so long that the girls had not only made tea but had each finished off a mug by the time I was able to talk with them again. They both seemed less upset, but still on edge.

"Your grandfather is coming here," I began. "The police will have lots of questions, and I know he wants to be with you."

Star still seemed stunned, and just nodded. Sunny looked confused and sat at the kitchen table with Paddy at her side. Just then we heard a car coming toward the house. It was good to have something to divert our attention. I looked out and saw a Sheriff's car slowing to a stop. A young African-American man in uniform and a solid older man in a gray suit got out and approached the house. I opened the front door before they reached it, and invited them inside.

The uniformed man introduced himself as Deputy Brown, and the other as Detective Dennis Milford. The deputy looked vaguely familiar, but I couldn't place him. I led them into the kitchen. Milford took charge and asked for the bracelet. Sunny still clutched it, but she held it out reluctantly. The younger man captured it in a plastic evidence bag he produced from somewhere and asked me to explain again how we had found the item.

I couldn't imagine there would be any useful fingerprints or clues on the bracelet, given years in the ground, a soggy trip in a dog's mouth, and then being wiped and held by three other people. However, I covered the basics of the afternoon's events once again.

Star tried to tell him that they were just playing with the dog when he ran off, almost out of their sight among the trees, started digging in the dirt and then began to bark.

"How are you related to these girls?" Milford interrupted.

"I'm not," I answered. "Their grandfather is on his way. He's their guardian. And Angelica's father."

"OK, we'll wait until he gets here."

Milford pulled Brown aside and said something to him, after which the deputy went out to the car, and the detective sat down heavily at the kitchen table and clamped his jaw shut. We sat there in uncomfortable silence.

The girls became tense and increasingly frightened at the man's gruff demeanor as the minutes ticked by. I was more than relieved when I heard another car approach. As soon as I said, "It's your grandfather," both girls jumped up and ran toward the front door.

After that, things began to get a little bit crazy. Len came inside with a girl hanging on each arm. He looked tired. He sat on the couch, still flanked by the girls, while they both talked at once, telling him about the afternoon. Detective Milford came into the living room and began to ask Len questions about Angelica that the girls had already answered. But he needed to hear the answers from an adult.

Meanwhile, I heard more vehicles outside, and stepped out on the porch. Another Sheriff's car pulled up, with two more deputies, followed by the Cherry Hill Police SUV. I was more than pleased to see Chief Tracy Jarvi, with Tom Baker, whom she sometimes deputized when extra help was needed. I went out to meet them. Tracy has a rugged Scandinavian build, coupled with a gentle manner that inspires confidence, making anyone who needs help feel safe.

"Tom, Tracy! I'm certainly glad to see you," I said. "But I thought you didn't have jurisdiction here."

"Remember, the law-enforcement services help each other out on big cases," said the Chief.

"So far, it doesn't seem as if the detective even believes this means anything at all," I blurted out.

"Oh, he does. Did Milford come, himself?"

"He's inside."

"Don't worry. He's not very personable, but he's competent."

"That's good to know."

"I guess we're gonna be lookin' for a body," Tom chimed in. Tom is my friend Cora's son. His English isn't good, and he always speaks too loudly because he is partially deaf.

Tracy put her hand on his arm and motioned for him to tone it down. "The girls are here. They're probably upset enough."

We went inside and quickly learned that Milford was getting people organized for a search of the swamp. He wasn't happy that he needed the girls to show him where they had been, and he wasn't happy at all that the dog might be the only one who really knew exactly where the bracelet had come from. Thankfully, he realized that Len would never be able to walk into the woods, but Len assured him that he would trust me to accompany his granddaughters. I wasn't sure this was an honor I wanted to accept for such a potentially gruesome job, but I knew it was something I would have to do.

By the time everyone was organized for a search, it was late afternoon. But summer evenings are long here, and I knew we might be facing several hours of walking through the edges of Dead Mule Swamp. Detective Milford asked me to put Paddy on a short leash. When he found out that Sunny, a ten-year-old, had been closest to the dog when the bracelet was found, he was even less pleased. He didn't seem to have much confidence in any of the resources he had been provided. He sent Star back to the house to stay with her grandfather and Deputy Brown, and she didn't seem sorry at being left out.

The ground was firm near the yard, so there was no chance of finding footprints there. We had to either trust that Sunny might recognize where she had gone, or hope that an untrained puppy would figure out that he was supposed to lead us to something he had found.

Nevertheless, within a few more minutes, Sunny, Milford, Paddy and I were walking into the woods to the northeast of my house, with two officers, plus Tracy and Tom, following like ducklings in a row.

15

We'd been instructed not to fan out yet, not until Sunny thought we were near where the dog had been digging. The detective didn't want to scuff up the area until we were more sure of what we were looking for.

Sunny started out with a lot of confidence. She knew she had followed what was probably a deer trail for some distance until it passed by a large cedar tree. She said she had climbed the tree and watched Paddy for a while from a low-hanging curved branch. From that perch she had picked another landmark, a white birch tree with a double trunk that was deeper into the woods on a little knoll. We hiked to the birch tree, and this also took us closer to open water in the swamp. We couldn't see the water yet, but the ground was becoming soft in low spots.

Beyond the birch tree, Sunny wasn't sure where she had gone. She said she'd just followed the dog and forgotten about paying attention to where she was. I cringed when I heard this; I knew all too well that this area could be dangerous. But I'd never considered that the girls would go exploring off the trail. We were lucky one of them hadn't gotten lost.

Paddy and I were put in the lead, and I was instructed to let the dog show us the way. I tried to follow these instructions, but Paddy didn't seem to understand what was expected of him. He kept looking at me and falling into step beside me. We'd been working on the "heel" command and it was associated in his mind with the leash. We weren't leading the way to anywhere.

"All right," barked Detective Milford. "We'll spread out from this tree. Did you go toward the water from here?" he asked

Sunny.

"We must have, because Paddy was right near the edge of some deep water when he was digging."

"That's helpful, at least," Milford admitted. "Stay in groups of two, but I'll keep the girl and the dog with me."

I assumed I was included with the dog. We continued straight east, while the two Sheriff Deputies veered southeast. Tracy and Tom angled to the northeast. We walked silently for a few minutes, until Sunny said, "I don't remember this place at all."

We had reached the edge of some open water with standing dead trees breaking from the surface and clawing at the sky. There was a small island about a hundred yards away. On the shore, practically at our feet, was a small broken rowboat, turned bottom-up. It had once been painted red, but was now weathered and mostly gray. I had no idea there was water deep enough to float any sort of boat so near my house. I had assumed any ponds were very shallow backwaters, but I now realized we must have come close to the river itself. Sunny was curious about the boat and while she looked it over I scanned the shore and saw a rectangle of old cement blocks that could have been the foundation for a tiny cabin. I wondered if we were still on my land or in the State Forest.

Far to our left I heard Tom's voice, almost a bellow. "... here. ...dog tracks," were the only words we could make out.

"Good." Detective Milford clipped the word, but he looked pleased as he began to stride north along the water's edge. We followed. "Where does the State Forest land start in here, Ms. Raven?" he asked.

"I'm not sure. I haven't had time to explore over this way yet. I own a strip all the way to the river, but we may be north of it, now, and I didn't know anything about that little camp back there."

The ground was becoming softer the farther we walked, and we passed a wooden stake pounded in the ground with orange flagging tape tied around the top. Milford stopped to look at it. There was lettering on the wood done with permanent marker, and he read, "'NE CORNER RAVEN.' Guess the camp is yours. This isn't." He lifted an arm in the direction we were heading. "Now we've got to call in the DNR."

He pulled out a cell phone and pushed some buttons. I thought he was calling the Department of Natural Resources directly, but instead I heard him say, "Chris? Yeah, come north. Send Paul back to the car to radio in and find out how we contact the DNR folks on Saturday. We're probably on state land." He clapped the phone shut and jammed it back in his pocket.

We heard Tom yell again, and we walked toward the voice. Suddenly, Sunny said, "I was here, I've seen that funny branch." She pointed to a tree with a limb that must have been bent in some ice storm years ago. "Paddy was over there." She pointed toward the water. The dog perked up his ears.

Now we could see Tom and Tracy, who were walking toward the water. We were following the crumbling sandy bank, and both our groups would soon converge at one place. Paddy began to whine and pull at the leash.

"Don't let him loose," growled Milford. "Who knows how much damage has been done already." He seemed to realize what might be about to happen and stopped suddenly. "You and the girl stay here."

I did not want to be left out of the discovery phase of this project, but I didn't want Sunny to be confronted with some gruesome find that might haunt her for the rest of her life, either. We stood still and waited.

I watched Tom, Tracy and Milford join forces. They pointed to the ground. I could see some raw, eroded sand near the water line. The downpour we'd had last Sunday might have caused some sort of washout which had exposed something. Milford and Tracy squatted down and moved their hands around as if they were casting some sort of spell. It was strange to watch with no accompanying words. Tom pulled a roll of yellow police tape out of his pocket and began stringing it between trees.

"What are they doing?" asked Sunny.

"That means they've found something that is important, and they are marking an area they want people to stay out of."

"What will they do next?"

"It depends on what they've found. We'll have to wait some more."

"I have to go to the bathroom. I usually just go in the woods, but there are a lot of men around here."

"OK, let me see if we can go home." I was glad enough to have a reason to leave. Staying there without being allowed to participate left me feeling completely useless. "Detective," I called.

Milford returned to where we were. He motioned me to one side. I handed Paddy's leash to Sunny and told her to hold him tightly. He said to me, "We definitely have a body. Just a skeleton—been here a long time, but it's arranged neatly; it was buried on purpose. Something disturbed an arm, probably the dog getting that bracelet. Can you take the little girl back to your house?"

"I think we can manage," I answered.

"Don't let the Leonards go home yet. I'll have more questions."

"All right. What should I tell Len?"

"The truth. Just keep in mind we don't know anything about whose remains these are, for sure."

Sunny and I easily found our way back. We passed the officer named Chris and told him to just keep going and he'd find the others. Sunny handed Paddy's leash to me and then took my hand, like a small child. She was quiet until we reached the white birch tree.

"It's my mother, isn't it?"

"We can't be sure yet, but I'm afraid it might be. How does that make you feel?"

"Kinda scared. I never thought about her much. She's just always been gone, but now it feels like she's everywhere."

I didn't have anything to add to this, so I squeezed her hand and we continued on to the house.

16

I told Len and Star, as gently as I could, that there was definitely a body in the swamp and after that, casual conversation never had a chance. Evening was coming on. Paddy curled up in his kennel without being told to. Deputy Brown went outside. Apparently we weren't being kept under close watch.

Finally, Star said, "I'm hungry."

Len said he hadn't had dinner either, and I assured them that there was plenty of food, although it would be pretty much the same as lunch. We busied ourselves making sandwiches, and fortified the leftover salad with more lettuce. Star boiled water so we could have tea with the light meal. Although we thought we were hungry, after the food was fixed no one felt like eating very much of it.

Deputy Brown and the one named Paul who was sent back to summon the DNR remained outside in one of the cars.

Just as the last of the light was fading, Detective Milford walked in the kitchen door. He seemed to have taken over the house as his base.

"Mr. Leonard, let's go in the living room," he said. It wasn't an invitation; it was a command.

Len nodded and stood up stiffly with the aid of his cane. The men left the kitchen, and I looked at the girls. They both looked very tired.

"Could we come to church with you tomorrow, if Grandpa says it's OK?" asked Star.

"Of course," I said.

"I know we haven't gone much, but I think it would make

me feel better."

"Me too," added Sunny. "I like the singing. I remember that. It made me happy."

"Did you used to go to Crossroads Fellowship?" I asked, surprised.

"Sometimes," Star explained. "Grandma liked to go. She was friends with some lady there, but it was easier to stay home than to drive into town. Most of the time she just watched church on television."

Len returned to the kitchen. "We can go home now," he said quietly.

"Can we go to church with Miss Ana tomorrow?" Sunny asked.

He looked at me, a bit pointedly, I thought. "Is she asking you to go?"

"No, Grandpa!" said Star. "I started it. I want to go like we did with Grandma. You come, too. OK?"

"I guess so. Sure. It might be a good idea, at that." I could almost see the struggle inside him, understanding that the girls wanted to make things be like old times, while he knew that it would never be the same again, given the reality that Angie could never return. He'd obviously always hoped, no matter how unlikely, that she might come home. "We'll drive into town. Service is at eleven?"

I nodded. "I'll meet you outside if you'd like."

"Good, we'll sit together. Now, let's go home and get some sleep."

Detective Milford was waiting in the living room. I had been able to see him over Len's shoulder, and was thankful that he didn't feel the need to barge in until the Leonards left. Then he told me what would be happening over the next few hours.

"We've got a DNR officer on the way here, with lights and a generator. We'll probably be working all night, coming and going. It'll be disruptive for you, but this is the closest access for vehicles. We have to remove the body, such as it is, and preserve any evidence that might be left. I want to get that done before word starts getting around. Seems silly to hurry after seven years, but curious people do strange things. Of course, there's little chance we'll find very much of value. It could be anyone, but at this point we're assuming it's Angelica

Leonard."

"Do you think it is?"

"Probably. The body's female, about the right size. There's the bracelet. Not much chance that's a coincidence, since there were only three of them, and the other two are accounted for. I can't say officially, of course. Forensics will have to study it."

"I understand."

"What else do you know about this?"

I explained that I knew next to nothing, since I'd only lived here for three months, and had known the Leonards for two weeks. I offered to leave the kitchen light on and the door unlocked so the officers could come in to get drinks or use the bathroom during the night.

Milford thanked me for that and let the screen door slam behind him as he left.

Paddy must have been startled by the noise of the door, because he woke up and came into the kitchen. I put him on his leash and took him outside for a minute. Then, after I set out some mugs, teabags, instant coffee, cocoa mix and a package of cookies, we climbed the stairs and I slipped into my pajamas. I thought I'd have trouble getting to sleep, and was planning to make a mental list of things I might say to the Leonards, and things I probably shouldn't say. But I fell asleep almost as soon as I lay down.

When I awoke, sun was streaming in the window, and Paddy's head was resting on my ankles. One foot was asleep. I hadn't heard a thing all night.

"Off," I muttered at the dog while trying to wiggle my dead foot.

"Oof?" Paddy yawned and jumped off the bed. My foot began to tingle as I tried to focus on the clock with my sticky morning eyes. Fortunately, I hadn't overslept.

When I let Paddy out, I saw that all the police cars were gone, except for one. The cookie package was empty, and several mugs had been placed in the sink. Three greasy pizza boxes were stacked on the counter. There was no one in sight, either in the kitchen or outside. I wondered if someone had been ordered to stay at the location in the woods, but since no one had appeared by the time I needed to leave, I could only guess.

"Sorry I was grumpy, earlier," I told Paddy, scratching his ears and rubbing his shoulders. "But you have to go in your kennel, anyway." I shut him in and drove into town.

I arrived at Crossroads Fellowship just a few minutes before the Leonards and was glad I had gotten there first, thinking it might be awkward for them to have to wait for someone they knew. I was aware that several church members listened to their police scanners with as much devotion as they listened to Sunday sermons. It was a near certainty that half the congregation had already heard what happened yesterday, and that the rest would know before dinnertime. I hoped churchgoers would be as tactful and kind as they should be, but I suspected I couldn't count on it.

Len, Star and Sunny all smiled when they saw me standing at the bottom of the steps which led to the peaked oak door of the white church. We went in together and chose a pew about halfway down the aisle, but nearer the left side than the middle.

One thing I liked about the church building was that it wasn't too plain, but neither was it too ornate. There was lovely old woodwork set off by the cream-colored walls, and the windows were stained glass, but geometric patterned, not fussy with Bible scenes.

Several people whom I hadn't previously met came over and said hello before the service started. One lady introduced herself as Beatrice Lindstrom. Len seemed particularly pleased to see her, and told me that she had been Becky's good friend.

"The two busy Bs, we called ourselves," she said with a little twitter. "Is it true they've found Angie?" The question might have seemed nosy from a casual acquaintance, but I could hear the genuine concern in her voice.

"Probably," said Len with a catch in his voice. "We have to wait for an autopsy to be sure, but I know it's her." He touched his heart.

"I'm so sorry," Beatrice said. "Call me if I can help. I really mean that."

"I will. Thank you."

"You girls have grown so much!"

Star wrinkled her nose, but Sunny said, "I'll be in sixth grade this fall!"

"My goodness. How about you?"

Politely, Star answered, "I'll be a sophomore."

"Oh! There's the pastor. We'll talk later." Beatrice patted Star on the arm and scurried to find her seat.

The music was a mixture of old hymns and some newer worship songs that I was just beginning to learn. Clearly, my companions weren't such guests as I had thought they would be, as they sang more of the words than I did. Except for the past month, I hadn't attended a church for years. I was surprised to learn that Len had an excellent baritone voice. There was a greeting time in the middle of the service, and several more people came over to say hello, including some young people, which made the girls happy. During the sermon, Sunny snuggled up against me and when I looked down at her once she smiled at me in a shy and secretive kind of way.

Afterwards, there was a lot of milling about during coffee time in the fellowship hall. People came and said hello to Len, others chatted with Star and Sunny. One man was hanging back, waiting to speak to us privately, and I suddenly realized why Deputy Brown had looked familiar the night before. I'd seen him every Sunday that I'd been coming here. There were a few African-Americans who attended this church, but I hadn't known he was in law enforcement. His eyes were red, and I wondered if he'd had any sleep.

When other people had drifted away he approached. "I just wanted to say how sorry I am... me personally," he began.

"Thank you, and thank you for waiting with Star and me last night," Len said.

"I had to be professional then, but I wanted to tell you that DuWayne and me were in the same class. We weren't real close, but we grew up in the same neighborhood. The whole thing is a damn shame. Excuse my French in church, but it is."

Len nodded. "I called DuWayne this morning. He does stay in touch enough that I have a current phone number."

"Is he gonna come?"

"Yes, he's on his way. He'll be here tomorrow. I think we'll have some kind of memorial service. It's not clear that we'll ever have a body to bury. Detective Milford said it's almost certainly... not... a natural death. And since it was so long ago, they'll need to keep everything for evidence. 'Cold cases don't get solved quickly,' he told me."

Brown turned his shoulder and said, "Excuse me, ladies." He began to whisper in Len's ear, but I heard most of what he said. "There were knife marks on a couple of ribs. We could see that, real clear, when we packaged up the remains. Did any of her friends carry a big knife?"

Len squinted but didn't answer the question; he looked like he had a headache. Between the events of the past day and sitting for an hour on a hard, narrow pew, I was sure he was experiencing more than one kind of pain.

"Thanks for letting me know, Harvey," Len said, purposely turning to include us again. Now I knew Deputy Brown's first name. "I'll try to remember anything I can about the week before she disappeared. You know, I was never asked very much about it, back then."

"I know, brother. It's hard to get respect, sometimes. Take care of those beautiful children." He shook hands with each of us, and left.

I offered to take us out to lunch, but Len said he really needed to go home and lie down for a while. He walked out to his car slowly, leaning heavily on his cane. The girls each gave me a little hug, and Sunny said she would call me when their dad arrived, so I could meet him. As I helped Len into his car, Star turned and said, "I'm glad we came. Sometimes people don't know what to say to us, because we're different, you know. But I can tell they care, even when they do dumb stuff like pat me on the arm. Thanks for everything."

17

Monday morning, Sunny phoned to tell me her father had arrived late Sunday night. She said he was planning to spend some time with them and she and Star wouldn't be able to work on their sewing projects until he had gone home again. She didn't sound either pleased or unhappy, but oddly indifferent, as if she were discussing the weather.

I called Adele at the store to find out if there was going to be a meeting of the Family Friends committee soon. Justin Gorlowski, Robert's nephew, answered the phone. He was working at the grocery for the summer months. I learned that Adele had gone on a trip to check out a possible produce supplier, and wouldn't be home until Wednesday. From this I deduced that there would be no committee meeting earlier than Thursday, and that Justin must have come a long way in understanding the grocery business since I had watched him bumble through his first few days at the store, back in May.

At long last, I assembled a dog travel kit and put towels, blankets, a filled water jug, the new bowl, a brush, an extra leash, plastic bags, a couple of balls, some treats and a plastic container of food into a large carton and stowed it in the back of the Jeep. It took up almost as much room as the dog himself.

It appeared that I had the rest of the day free, and I knew just how I was going to use the time. After taking Paddy for a short walk down my familiar trail, I clipped him on his cable run and drove in to Cherry Hill to Jouppi's Hardware to look at paint samples. I returned with primer, ceiling paint, and several gallons of a buttery off-white paint that wasn't quite yellow, but looked very rich. A handful of color cards displaying shades from seafoam green to teal were jammed in my back pocket. I was toying with painting one end wall a bright color.

None of the window trim was in place yet, and only the subfloor was laid, so it was a perfect time to paint. I didn't have to worry about splatters very much at all. By late afternoon I had finished the primer coat, and two coats of ceiling paint. I washed the brushes and rollers. Paddy was anxious to go out, and I was hungry, having skipped lunch. It had been a quiet day, and I appreciated the respite from all the activity of the weekend. I was in the kitchen, making a sandwich and stretching my sore neck muscles when Paddy began to bark from the driveway.

I looked out the window and saw Star coasting into the yard on a bicycle. She looked like a woman on a mission, not like a carefree teenager. I opened the door just as she was stepping onto the porch, and she stamped into the living room, followed by Paddy.

"Hi there!" I said. "Come in the kitchen and have a drink. I'm just eating. Would you like something?"

"Just some water. Can we talk? I'm so angry at my dad I could... I could... I don't know what, but he just doesn't understand."

"Did you ride all the way here? It must be fifteen miles."

"I just couldn't stand it any longer! It was the only way I could get away. Poor Sunny is stuck there, but she said she'd be OK and that I should come tell you."

"What's happening?" I led the way into the kitchen, and poured Star a glass of cold water from a pitcher in the refrigerator, trying not to look alarmed. We sat at the kitchen table.

"It's Dad."

"What's the matter? Did he hurt you?"

She took a long drink of water. "No, no. He's not like that. I know he's our dad, but he thinks he runs everything, when he hasn't even seen us since Grandma's funeral."

"Tell me about it."

"First of all, he acts like he owns the place. The trailer is small, you know. He has to sleep on the couch when he comes. Maybe it just bothers me more, now that I'm older, but he seems to fill up all the space. The recliner section of the couch is the only place Grandpa can sit and be comfortable, but Dad slept late, and then didn't fold up his blankets. So Grandpa had to sit on a hard chair till Dad got up, and then Grandpa had to fold up the blankets himself, just to be able to have his place to sit."

DuWayne's behavior sounded rather thoughtless to me, but hardly serious enough to have caused Star to ride her bicycle all the way to my house. I took a bite of sandwich and Star went on with her tale.

"Then he used up all the hot water taking a shower, and ordered me to make breakfast for him. I would've fixed his old breakfast, you know. I just didn't like being told to do it, like I was his slave or something."

"I can understand that," I said.

"I guess this kind of stuff is nothing new, but it made me so mad, on top of the other things he said."

"Like what?"

Star squirmed in her chair. "He wasn't very nice."

"In what way?" I was hoping that offering a listening ear was going to be sufficient help, because I had no interest in interjecting myself into a family argument. From what Len had told me, DuWayne didn't even have parental rights, legally.

"It's like he doesn't care about Mom. He said that we should have known she must be dead. But, why wouldn't we want to dream that she might come back? I remember what it was like when we were together." She sighed and finally slowed down the pace of her rant. "A little bit anyway."

"Were things good for you, back then?"

"I guess we must have been really poor, but I didn't know it. I remember Dad being big and warm. He would hold us on his knees and give us horsey rides. Sunny would giggle and giggle, but I had to hold on tight because he bounced me harder since I was older. We would go to town for baby-size soft ice cream cones, and watch the sun set from our porch."

"Were you hoping things could be like that again?"

"Not really, oh, maybe a little bit... I've been thinking a lot this year, I guess. Mom was just a year older than I am when she had me. I pretty much take care of things for us since Grandma died, but I can't imagine doing all that and having a baby, too."

"Your mom must have worked very hard."

Star changed the direction of her story. "Sunny and I walked down to our old trailer earlier this year. She didn't remember it at all."

"But you did?"

"Some things. I remember it being bigger. We used to chase each other up and down the hall. That Sunny could run even when she was a toddler! Now, when she runs inside our trailer I tell her to stop. The whole place shakes. Living in a trailer is really crappy."

"You keep yours very clean and nice."

"Thanks. I try, but we have some money from when Grandpa got hurt. I don't think my mom had anything at all. That's why she was trying to get that job. At least now I know that she didn't walk away and leave us."

"Did you think that, before?"

"I didn't want to think so, but sometimes I would hear people talking, until they thought I might hear them, and then they clammed up. It was hard, not knowing. But now, I know she couldn't come back and that means she really loved us. Right up until the end." Tears began to run down her cheeks.

"I don't want to get your hopes up, but we don't know for certain yet that it is your mom."

"Yes we do. The Sheriff called a while ago and said the dental records proved it. Grandpa is planning a memorial service for Wednesday."

"I'm so sorry," I said, feeling inadequate.

"I have to be strong for Sunny and Grandpa, but would it sound like a kid to ask for a hug?"

"Of course not!" We stood up and I held Star close while she cried silently.

"Grandpa's really sad, and he's letting Dad boss him around."

"You've lost your mother, but he's lost a daughter, too. I think he'll be fine, but it will take some time. Your grandfather is a good man."

We heard a diesel truck coming into the driveway.

"That's Dad," said Star, pulling away from me and running to the window. "How did he know I was here? Sunny must've told him."

This was going to be awkward. It wasn't exactly the way I had hoped to meet DuWayne Jefferson, but that couldn't be helped now. He walked purposefully toward the porch and seemed prepared to pound on the door, but I opened it before he had a chance. I wanted to take the initiative.

"Hi Dad," Star said.

"Hello, Mr. Jefferson," I said at the same time.

The man never looked at me, but glared at Star. "What are you doing here?"

"I came over to talk to Miss Ana," she answered. Her voice was firm, but not as confident as I knew it could be.

"Get in the truck," DuWayne ordered. "And put your bike in the back, first."

"Yes, sir."

I stepped back, and Star pushed past DuWayne and walked meekly toward her bicycle.

DuWayne turned to me. He was, indeed, a big man, probably six feet tall. He was solid and muscular with a shaved head, and he was wearing a tight black t-shirt and black pants. I'm not easily intimidated, but I certainly wouldn't ever want to cross this man. Nevertheless, I didn't appreciate his brusque manner with a young girl who had just figured out that she'd lost her mother and somehow grown up without a childhood, especially when that girl was his daughter and should have been able to count on some sympathy from him.

"I don't like you messing with my family," he said in a cold voice. "Those girls have a hard enough time as it is without someone making them think they're better than they are."

"I'm not sure what you mean—we've made cookies and are sewing some school clothes. Those aren't exactly extravagant."

"And I've heard about you solving mysteries. I've been here one day, and already people tell me you poke your nose into other people's problems."

I was shocked. "Look, I have nothing to do with this. Angelica was buried along the river, and my driveway provides good access. I enjoy spending time with the girls, but I'm certainly not going to try to solve a seven-year-old murder."

"Good. And while I'm here, the girls won't need you. Got it?"

I looked up at him and took a deep breath. "I understand you are upset that Star came over here without permission. I'm perfectly willing to keep in the background, but young girls need a woman around, sometimes. Please don't punish Star. Naturally, she's upset by everything that's happened and needed to talk about her mother."

"We'll see. And you keep that mutt away from us, too." He pivoted on his heel and marched back to the big black truck. As he did a K-turn and spun out of the yard it looked as if he was yelling at Star, and she was hugging the passenger door, trying to move as far from her father as she could.

Paddy had been crouched at my feet, growling softly in his throat, apparently trying to understand the angry human voices he was unaccustomed to hearing. I'd almost forgotten him. Now he stood up and nuzzled my hand. Suddenly my knees were weak, and I collapsed into an easy chair. The dog put his head in my lap.

"Now what, Paddy?" I asked, as I stroked his silky ears.

18

There wasn't much I could do about any of it. I hoped I'd be welcome at the memorial service on Wednesday; I couldn't imagine that Len would uphold DuWayne's wish that I stay away from the girls. Meanwhile, the next day was Tuesday, my regular day to spend with Cora. I said a little prayer that DuWayne wouldn't upset Star and Sunny too much, and went to bed early with a copy of Bleak House. I thought a few chapters about the machinations of a broken legal system would make the Leonards' situation look much brighter. The sun was not even all the way down when I fell asleep, a victim of hard work, high emotions and Dickens.

When Paddy and I arrived at Cora's the next day, I thought she looked like the proverbial cat that had swallowed the canary. And I didn't have to wait long to find out why. Paddy settled down in the office, and she led me to one of the long work tables in the museum where there was an array of photographs and a couple of newspapers.

"Look what I dug out of the files for your new case!" Cora's enthusiasm was bubbling over.

"My new case? No way. I am not getting mixed up in this murder mystery. I just want to help Star and Sunny, not solve old crimes."

"If you say so, but look at these things anyway. They can give you more understanding of the Leonard family. I've laid them out chronologically." Cora was definitely grinning.

I leaned over the left end of the table and began to study the photos.

"Those are shots of Hammer Bridge Town when it was new and shiny," Cora explained. "The construction company paid people to move there. They also convinced Howard Donnelly to build that gas station and convenience store. Probably gave him a subsidy."

"What year was that?"

"1983."

"No wonder the trailers are in such bad shape now. Was Len on one of the construction crews?"

"Look at this picture." Cora pointed to a group photo in the next row. About twenty men were posed in front of a large bulldozer. Len was obviously the one seated on the machine. He was young and burly, but his long face was easily recognizable. Also in that row, Cora had placed a copy of the *Cherry Hill Herald* that carried the story of the opening of the new bridge. I read that the old bridge had become unsafe and Sheep Ranch Road had to be closed until construction was complete. Since it was a main route, a lot of people were inconvenienced, having to drive five miles south to cross the bridge on US 10.

I went back to the first row of pictures. There was one of the old bridge, a flimsy-looking thing with rusted, spidery railings. It looked like it should have been replaced long before 1983. There were several of various stages of construction, ending with a shot of the new bridge taken from a low angle, showing the beams in dramatic perspective. All of these photos were black and white, and looked professionally taken, but the next set consisted of colored snapshots of small groups seated at picnic tables, probably from someone's family album.

"Those are of the picnic given for the construction workers and their families after the bridge was done. It was held over at Turtle Lake. Can you find the Leonards?"

I squinted at the square photos, with their colors fading to muddy purplish hues. I finally found a grouping at a picnic table with a man, woman, and a girl who looked about four years old. They were seated with another couple who appeared to be a little younger, with a boy about the same age as the girl.

"Here?" I asked.

"You found them! Do you know who that is at the same table?"

"Not a clue." I thought about reminding her I'd lived in the area only a few months, but decided her question indicated acceptance of me into the fabric of the county rather than its being a set-up for failure.

"That's the Louamas—Marko, Judy and little Larry. He doesn't look like a terror in that picture, does he?"

"Not at all." I contemplated whether future criminals could be predicted by looking at their pre-school pictures. "So this is Becky? And Angelica? It's strange to think of them both being dead."

"Isn't it? Way too many people who are younger than I am are dead," Cora said with a trace of sadness.

"The Louamas live in Hammer Bridge Town?"

"Not now. They moved into Cherry Hill right after the bridge was finished. They're on the south end of Dogwood. It's not the best part of town, but they do own their own house."

In the next section Cora had placed newspapers covering Angelica's disappearance. As she had noted the week before, there wasn't much about it. It was as if the disappearance of a young woman, possibly entangled in the area's drug culture, was of no concern to anyone except her family. The paper ran a head shot of Angelica on the first day after the missing persons report had been filed. It was her senior picture, the one I had already seen. The following day an article detailed the search efforts made near Hammer Bridge, and along Sheep Ranch Road. Apparently, serious effort had been made to check the creek, because the water had been high in June that year, and there was some consideration given to the idea that she might have fallen or been pushed into the water. Interestingly enough, the photo with the article was a shot of the bridge taken from the same angle as the glossy from the bridge completion. I wondered if the photographer realized the duplication, or if perhaps it was just an accessible vantage point for photo taking. I squinted at the grainy newspaper graphic. There was something on the lower edge of one of the large beams.

"Have you got a magnifying glass?" I asked.

"Sure," said Cora, walking briskly to the desk and returning as fast as she could. "What have you found?"

"Get that other bridge picture, the one that looks like this one." I held the magnifier over the square-sided bump on the beam. There was a round shape on one face, but I couldn't make out what it was. Then I looked at the glossy photo, which was much more clear. There was no round bump, and no rectangular shape for it to be on. "You look. What do you think this is?"

Cora studied the photos. "It looks like a box of some sort, but I don't know what that round thing is. Some kind of decoration, maybe?"

"Have you ever heard about a box being found under the bridge, in connection with any local story?"

"No, but it was probably just some treasure hidden by small boys. Bridges make wonderful hideouts, you know."

"I know, but why don't we go see if it's still there? It's a beautiful day, and we would have fun looking."

"I thought you weren't getting involved in this case?"

"What are the chances this has anything to do with Angelica? It will take my mind off that whole mess."

"All right, I suppose it wouldn't hurt me to get out somewhere. Let's take our lunch and eat at Turtle Lake. If you pack up some food, I'll put these things away. You'll find a cooler in the porch."

By the time I got the food collected and Cora had returned the papers and photos to their files it was eleven o'clock. We decided to go to the park first. We didn't want to waste any time, so we just took the paved roads, crossing the county on School Section Road and turning north on Kirtland until we reached the turnoff to Turtle Lake. During the drive, I filled Cora in on my conversations with Star and DuWayne. She shared my concern for the girl, but her body language made it clear that she still didn't have much use for DuWayne.

At the Recreation Area, the first order of business turned out to be walking the dog who was whining and wiggling in the back seat.

We strolled across the dam and took the trail that followed the north shore of the lake, walking about twenty minutes before we turned around and headed back for the picnic area. I was glad I'd purchased the pack of bags that stayed clipped on the leash, or I would have forgotten to bring any with me. The trail was wide and well-maintained, not a place you'd want to leave evidence of dog-walking. While we walked, Cora told me about the valley that had been flooded to create the lake. At least it wasn't some sad tale of an entire town being wiped out and the residents dispossessed. Only one farmstead had been relocated, and that owner had sold out willingly.

Our picnic was enjoyable, but short. We didn't have all that much food with us and we weren't feeling childish enough to need the playground. It was hot sitting in the sun. As on the day I'd first been to this lake, there were kayaks near the islands, and the beach was obviously popular with families on hot summer days. I thought I might come for a swim some time. Then again, I wondered if the water was deep enough to swim where we'd found the old rowboat on my property, which was close enough for me to walk to from my house.

"Ready to explore?" I asked, licking brownie crumbs from my thumb.

"Let's go," Cora agreed. "I feel like a little girl on a scavenger hunt."

19

From Turtle Lake it was just over ten miles to Hammer Bridge, and we encountered only a few other cars.

"I'm glad we're coming in from the east, so we don't have to drive past the Leonards," I said.

"Stop worrying. They aren't wasting time watching the traffic on their road. It's a busy route."

"Probably, but I don't want to take a chance of annoying DuWayne. They might be outside on a nice day like this." I felt like we were being chancy enough, snooping around just a mile from the trailer.

When we reached the bridge, we pulled onto a wide shoulder on the southeast side. Obviously many people had parked here.

"That box is going to be long gone," Cora predicted.

"We'll know really soon," I countered.

As it turned out, it wasn't so easy to complete our quest. The embankments beneath the bridge were really steep, and had grown up with berry bushes since the pictures had been taken. It was almost twenty feet down to the water. In fact, it was hard to figure out just where we should be hunting. I had thought the pictures were taken looking to the east, and that the box was up under the bridge on that side of the creek. While I was trying to figure out how to scramble under the beams on the steep slope, Cora wandered off along the creek on the north side of the road. Paddy had already found a way down the steep slope and was splashing in the stream, trying to pull a branch from a pile of jumbled brush that had hung up on a fallen tree. The water was low and flowing gently, so I figured it was safe enough to let him play.

"Come see this," Cora called.

I wasn't having much luck finding any access, let alone an

easy one, and brushed the dirt off my jeans as I walked across the road, then pushed through some saplings, to join her on a small pointed bluff of land that defined an eastward bend in the creek.

"I think this is where those pictures were taken," she said. "Look at that rock. Isn't that in the photos?"

"Yes it is. The box should be over on those beams, then. Do you see it?"

"It's all covered with nightshade vines and nettles. That won't be much fun to crawl through."

"I've got a jacket in the car."

We crossed the bridge, but I stopped first to pull my nylon windbreaker from the back seat, slipping it on as we walked. On the northwest side of the bridge the vegetation was lush, but not as thick with berry bushes. With the jacket on to protect my arms from the stinging nettles it was fairly easy to slide a short way down the bank, where I discovered a narrow benched area in the slope on which I could stand. It led directly to the underside of the bridge. Making my way carefully so that the vines didn't trip me—it would be a nasty fall to the bottom—I continued until I could reach up and grab the metal of the bridge supports. The area where the box should be was so obscured with weeds that I couldn't tell, even yet, if the box was there. I searched for a stick to push the nettles aside, but couldn't find one.

Reluctantly, I pulled the sleeve of my jacket down over my hand, and used my arm to sweep the vines and stalks out of the way. There it was, a small rusty tackle box, pushed back against the concrete of the abutment. The round shape we had seen was a combination padlock, slipped through the hasp. Eagerly, I stretched on tiptoe to reach for it, and lost my footing just as my fingers closed around the corners of the box. I began sliding and crashing through the brush.

"What's happening? Are you all right?" I heard Cora call. I couldn't answer her. I was busy. Busy twisting so that I was sliding on my back instead of with my face against the bank. Busy holding the box so we wouldn't lose it. Busy trying to see where I was going to land. I caught a glimpse of Paddy looking up at me with an expression of absolute surprise on his face. He gave a sharp yip and leapt out of the way.

Where I landed, not surprisingly, was in the creek. The bank had been steep, but not sheer, and there were a number of small bushes that slowed my descent. I hoped I might just get wet shoes, but no such luck. My feet hit the water first, but the creek bed was uneven and I couldn't get my footing. I continued to slide until I was sitting flat on my bottom in the cool water, clutching the rusty, dusty box. I began to laugh. I laughed so hard I almost cried.

Cora apparently thought I was making sounds of distress. "Oh no," I heard her say. "Is anything broken? Can you get up? Shall I try to stop a car? Ana! Answer me!"

"I'm fine," I finally managed to call between gasps. Paddy had come to my aid and was busily licking my face. "Just wet. And I have our treasure box. Help me figure out how to get back up the bank."

Paddy also found the solution to that problem. When I told him to "Go find the car," he walked upstream in the water around the bend. Since I was already wet I simply followed him. There, we found a wide gully that met the creek, and we easily climbed up to the east bank.

"I'm over here!" I yelled as I emerged from the woods at the road edge, and Cora came back across the bridge to meet me. Now she was laughing. I crossed to the car and stood there dripping, causing small muddy puddles to form below the hem of my jeans.

"Oh, my! I haven't had so much fun in a coon's age. I mean... you are all right, aren't you?" She covered her mouth and tried to stop laughing, but we both ended up giggling like junior high schoolgirls.

Except for a few scratches on my hands and one ankle, I really was fine. It was a good thing I had packed two towels and two blankets since both Paddy and I needed them for the trip home. I handed the box over to Cora.

"Let's go to my place first, so I can get some dry clothes," I suggested.

"Of course," Cora agreed. I headed west, and she added, "I thought you didn't want to go past the Leonards."

"Too bad! I'm not stopping to visit, so for all they know I've been shopping in Emily City."

I kept my eyes on the road, but I was quite sure I heard

Cora trying to stifle more chuckles.

After reaching my house, I headed upstairs to change, and told Cora to make herself at home, and pour us some lemonade. When I returned to the kitchen the box was cleaned off and sitting on some paper towels in the middle of the table, flanked by two glasses of lemonade loaded with ice.

"What do you think?" I asked.

"Of our box?" Cora shrugged. "It could be something interesting, or it might be full of fishhooks and old bubblegum wrappers. Although I'm not sure little boys would have put a hefty combination lock like that on a tackle box."

"I was thinking that too. Should we break it open?"

Cora stared at the box as if it were radiotransmitting answers. "I think not just yet. Let's hold on to it for a while and think about it. I'll try to recall some other children who lived in that area in 2004. You have to wonder why it was left there, never reclaimed."

"Kids forget about things."

"Things they've locked up with a big padlock?"

"Good point."

We finished the lemonade, and I showed Cora around my house. She'd never been there, since she left her home very seldom. We chatted about colors and curtain styles, and she concluded that the house was going to look much nicer than when Jimmie Mosher had lived there. I suggested we might as well make the day complete and have an early dinner. We settled on the shabby but reliable Pine Tree Diner, in Cherry Hill, but Cora refused to let me pay for her meal. However she did agree to attend the memorial service for Angelica. And she took the padlocked tackle box when I dropped her at her home on Brown Trout Lane. I wondered if she planned to lock the box in the old bank safe where we had stored evidence about the Sorenson case.

20

The rest of Tuesday was uneventful but productive. I painted a little bit, but was interrupted by a call from Adele letting me know that the memorial service for Angelica was scheduled for eleven a.m. the next day, to be followed by a light luncheon. I passed that information on to Cora, and told her to expect me at ten-thirty, but she said Tom would pick her up, so that she'd be free to leave when she wanted. Adele had suggested I bring something, so I made a quick run into town and bought cucumbers, lemon gelatin, and cottage cheese to make one of my favorite molded salads. I also stopped at Jouppi's and picked up more accent-paint sample cards, this time in tones of wine and plum.

I spent a lot of time pondering what the atmosphere might be at the service. As it turned out, my imagined scenarios were wrong in nearly every way.

On Wednesday, I arrived at the church a bit early to deliver my salad, and just as I was emerging from the fellowship hall to cross into the auditorium, Cora and Tom entered the building. I joined forces with them, and we found seats toward the back, near the right side. A teenage usher handed us programs as we entered, and the organist was playing tunes I didn't recognize, but which seemed quite upbeat for funeral music. The pews weren't full, but there was a decent turnout. I was glad to see that people apparently wanted to be supportive. I studied the groups of people, and saw more than a few who seemed to be the same age as Angelica would have been, probable friends or classmates.

"That's Jordan and Kaitlyn Wilcox, up there," Cora said. She was following my eyes. "No, the ones farther right with the baby. Kaitlyn was in Angie's class. And so was Marty Ashton.

He's over there with his parents. Marty was special ed, but he's harmless." The man she indicated was pudgy and seemed to be sitting very close to his mother, for an adult. He turned, and I recognized the features of a person with Down Syndrome. For all the facts we had, almost anyone who knew Angelica might have been involved in her death, but I found it hard to suspect Marty.

Angelica's family was seated in the left front row. DuWayne and Len wore suits. I had to admit that DuWayne did not look at all like a thug when he was dressed up. He looked like a successful young businessman, although I had no idea what he really did for a living. The permanently uncomfortable angle of Len's back made his clothes fit poorly, with wrinkles in odd places, but when he turned to look over the room I could see that his shirt and suit had been pressed recently. He nodded and smiled at me.

This action made Sunny turn around. She wasn't smiling, but she waved at me in a subdued way. I waved back. Star seemed to be concentrating on something she held in her hands, and she wasn't paying attention to anyone else. The girls wore similar outfits, which had been true every time I'd seen them. For the service, they had chosen scoop-neck t-shirts in deep gold, and tiered peasant skirts in various subdued prints. Not identical, but very similar.

A few more people drifted in, including a young couple I didn't know, who took the pew right behind the Leonards and DuWayne Jefferson. The girl was dressed in a short, tight leather skirt, leather jacket, and high heels. She wore several gold chains and rings. The man also had on a leather jacket, and his black jeans were very tight. They certainly stood out in a room full of plainly dressed locals. Cora shook her head when I looked at her to silently ask their identities.

Detective Milford was there, accompanied by the deputy, Harvey Brown. Although by this time I knew that this was Harvey's regular church, he was in uniform, so his presence seemed official. They had staked out the very back row on the left, and it didn't look as if they would welcome company. Just at eleven, I looked around the room once more, and saw Chief Tracy Jarvi come in and take a seat with the other law enforcement personnel. Apparently she was not intimidated by

Milford.

Rev. Dornbaugh stood up and began the service. I discovered the program contained not only an order of worship, but also words to songs and readings in which we were expected to participate. Someone had put in a lot of time on this service over the past few days, or perhaps Len had been planning things for years, just in case.

We sang songs I'd never heard, which were identified as favorites of Angelica. One sounded like a restaurant billboard inviting worshippers to come as they are. Apparently, the Church had changed a lot during the years I'd been away; no one used to come just as they were. I thought one phrase of "Shine, Jesus, Shine" was especially pertinent: "Jesus, light of the world shine upon us, set us free by the truth you now bring us."[1] Angelica needed some truth going for her. I hoped Detective Milford or someone would be able to provide some answers.

There were predictable Scripture passages, offering words of hope to the living, and a traditional hymn, "Trust and Obey." The program said Len had chosen that one.

Next, Rev. Dornbaugh introduced Star and explained that she would be reading a poem of her own composition. Star took Sunny's hand and together they mounted the steps to the platform. Star seemed somewhat self-conscious, and Sunny stared at the floor. Then Star gained her composure, took the microphone and read from a card in her hand.

> Mommy Angel, we remember,
> Bedtime books and teddy bears,
> We will love you always,
> And be sure to say our prayers.
>
> If we have one wish for you,
> It's that Jesus is holding you tight.
> Your heavenly girls know you have
> A better home, in perfect light.
>
> Rest in peace, Star and Sunny.

She fumbled to replace the microphone in the stand, but the

pastor came and took it from her, giving her shoulder a squeeze as he did so. Then he touched Sunny on her shoulder, and she looked up at him with the same bland, confused expression I'd seen on her face since the body had been found.

After some brief words by Rev. Dornbaugh, the service ended with a prayer, and "Lead, Kindly Light," which the program indicated had been one of Becky's favorites. Then we were all dismissed to the fellowship hall for lunch. Angelica's family left the auditorium first, with the pastor. I waited and watched, as other attendees filed down the center aisle. Detective Milford and company stood silent and scowling, carefully studying each person who had come to pay respect.

When Cora, Tom, and I got to the vestibule, Angelica's family was standing in a line so that people could walk past them and say a word or two of condolence. I saw Sunny whisper something to her grandfather, and he nodded in return. When we reached them Sunny said to me, "Sit with us, OK?"

I looked at Len, and he added, "Please do." I felt awkward, since I was with Cora and Tom, but I should have realized Cora had already spent enough time with a group of people. Tom was shaking hands with DuWayne, but he didn't speak, perhaps aware that he spoke too loudly in church.

Cora said appropriate things to Len, Star and Sunny, and even shook DuWayne's hand stiffly. Then she excused herself, took Tom's arm and they headed for the exit.

"I'll join you when you're done here," I said to Len. I smiled at the girls and continued to the fellowship hall. Adele motioned for me to help set out foods, so that gave me something to do while the Leonards were busy.

"Did you see the Ybarras?" she whispered as soon as I came into the kitchen.

"Who are they?"

"I can't believe they had the nerve to show up at church!"

"Adele, who are they? Why shouldn't they come?"

"Those kids that sat behind the Leonards."

"Kids? They looked like adults to me."

"Oh, sure, but they were kids with Angie. They're brother and sister, Pablo and Juanita."

"Well, it's nice that some of her friends came."

"Not those kinds of friends! Don't you know what she was messing around with?" Adele rolled her eyes. "That's what happens when we have to skip meetings where we can talk. You probably don't know. They were all dealing drugs, but our law enforcement was so terrible back then that they never got caught by anyone who mattered. Most of us just tried to stay out of their way."

"Actually, I've heard some of that story. Didn't they hang out with Larry Louama?"

"That's a fact. That boy is nothing but trouble! Thank goodness he's in prison now. One less scumbag to worry about."

"That's not very nice."

"I don't care. He was getting to the point of... uh oh... here they all come. Better get out there and be friendly."

I shook my head and left the kitchen. Sunny ran over and grabbed my hand, then led me to the table where her sister and grandfather were just sitting down. DuWayne was working his way toward us, bringing the Ybarras with him.

"Len, I think you know these folks," he began. Len struggled to turn and shake hands before committing his weight to the seat. He tripped on the legs of the metal folding chair, and almost fell. I could see that he was very tired, and also noted DuWayne didn't reach out to steady the older man. "Girls, and Ms. Raven, these are old friends of mine, Pablo and Juanita Ybarra." He looked at Star and Sunny, and added pointedly. "They were friends with your mom, too."

The girls didn't seem to know what to say, but sat there in awkward silence. The unpleasant DuWayne had changed like a chameleon to become personable.

"We were very sorry to learn that Angelica was really dead," Pablo said.

"Yes, it's such a shame. But perhaps it's good to know." echoed his sister.

"It's nice to meet you," I said. "Do you live around here now?"

"I'm in Detroit," said Juanita. "Pablo still lives in Emily City."

"What do you do?"

Pablo answered first. "I'm a manager at Pizza Plus."

"I'm in sales," added Juanita.

"Oh, what do you sell?"

"Fad-fueled, big-ticket items to people with too much money and time." She flashed me a white smile from her perfectly made-up face, and laughed, but with little humor.

Neither of them asked me any questions, and I wasn't sure what else to say, but it didn't matter. The serving line had started and Sunny pointed and pulled on my arm.

"Would you like me to bring you a plate?" I asked Len.

"That would be very kind," he said.

We all shuffled over to the serving table, and the Ybarras joined the line behind me. Detective Milford materialized from somewhere and imposed himself beside the Ybarra siblings. They glanced at him, but seemed to be missing the intimidating signals he was sending. As I headed back toward Len, juggling two large plates and two dessert plates, I noticed that the detective hadn't moved ahead in the line. I thought he must still be making sure that everyone knew they were under scrutiny, by virtue of his presence.

I made it to the table safely with all the plates, and Len was content with the food choices I had made for him. The rest of our time at the church was spent eating, or listening to DuWayne, Juanita and Pablo making small talk about events from the past. They seemed to have a lot of private jokes that set off laughs, smirks and high-fives. The rest of us were not exactly uncomfortable, but the focus had definitely moved off Len and the girls.

I told Star how much I enjoyed her poem and that I thought she was courageous to read it during the service. She looked pleased. Sunny nudged me under the table, and when I looked at her she took a deep breath. But when she spoke, it wasn't to me.

"Dad, I think Grandpa needs to go home and rest. Can we leave now?"

To DuWayne's credit, he looked at Len with some compassion. The older man was practically shaking with the effort to remain somewhat upright without leaning on the table.

"Sure, Sunshine. Let's go." The words were right, but DuWayne always sounded slightly angry to me.

Star ran around the table to help Len stand, and DuWayne

turned to say goodbye to his friends who were also on their feet and seemed anxious to leave. Sunny pulled me down to her level.

"Dad's leaving tomorrow afternoon. I'm really glad," she whispered.

- - - - - -

1. Used with permission. Graham Kendrick ©1987 Make way Music. www.grahamkendrick.co.uk

21

After the Leonards and DuWayne left, things wound down quickly. A few stragglers were still eating, but they soon brought their plates to the pass-through to the kitchen and then headed for the exit. The ladies' group prided itself on using real plates and silverware for funeral lunches. I grabbed one of the spare aprons, tied it over my dress, and began washing dishes. Adele was bustling about wiping off tables, so I chatted with several other people who were helping to tidy the kitchen.

When the dishes were done, I saw Adele deep in conversation with a large young man, and an older man who was nearly bald, neither of whom I recognized. I'd met enough new people for one day, and scooted for my car while I had the chance.

Paddy was more than happy to see me when I arrived home. He hadn't spent such a long time in his kennel since he'd come to stay with me.

"How about a walk?" I asked him. "I need some exercise too." I changed clothes and got us each a fresh drink of water.

Now that I knew about the former cabin on my property I was really curious. I wondered if it might be possible to put a canoe in the river there and paddle up to the dam. The water wasn't fast-moving at this time of year, and the ruined rowboat seemed to indicate that some previous owner might have visited the island.

Paddy ran free, although I took his leash along, just in case we encountered a porcupine or something. We followed the route Sunny had led us on before: take the deer path to a large cedar, jog to the white birch and then head straight east to the water.

However, when we got to the white birch, I felt drawn, instead, to the northeast, toward Angelica's grave site. I hadn't been there since the body had been discovered. The police seemed to be finished; my driveway provided the closest vehicle access, and I hadn't seen an official car since Tuesday. It was no trouble at all finding the way. The ground was softer here, and so many officers and technicians had been back here since Saturday that a path was well trampled.

Nearing the water, I knew I was getting close because the yellow crime-scene tape was strung through the trees. I was surprised to see it still in place, feeling pretty sure that there was no one assigned to guard the site.

A light wind lifted the leaves, and on the breeze came the smell of fresh cigarette smoke. Maybe I was mistaken.

"Hello," I called. "Anastasia Raven here. Who's on duty?" I reached down and grabbed Paddy's collar, and clipped him to the leash. If the site was being protected, I knew they didn't want a dog disturbing things. Fastening the dog only took a couple of seconds, but I was surprised when no one answered.

"Hello!" I tried again, louder this time. I was also closer by now. Surely the officer had heard me. But the only sounds were the rustling of leaves and a slight gurgling from where the river bent and water slapped against a fallen log.

I reached the grave site. The smell of burning tobacco was strong here, but there was no one in sight. It looked to me as if the police were finished, since the grave had been filled in, leaving a large area of raw dirt but no gaping hole. Oddly, there were footprints all over the bare area. It took me a couple of seconds to react to the fact that the prints had been made by someone wearing high-tech athletic shoes with swirling patterns and a nipped waist between the ball and heel, and were not the marks of the dress shoes or work boots the official visitors wore. The impressions were also very fresh. Suddenly, the quiet in the woods seemed unfriendly. No birds flitted from branch to branch, and just then a small cloud moved across the sun, deadening the sunny day. I shivered involuntarily.

I tried to sort out the tracks. I hadn't seen any with this distinctive pattern on the well-used path I'd taken to this location. Then I realized they both came from and led toward the water. A blue jay screeched in anger from a distance upstream and Paddy began barking frantically and tugging against the leash.

"Who's there?" I yelled, but I doubted I could be heard over the din the dog was making. "You're on private property." I was pretty sure whoever it was had crossed over the boundary line to my land by that time. I released the dog. "Go get him, Paddy," I said.

This wasn't a command we'd worked on, but I was sure it was what Paddy had in mind anyway. He ran along the water's edge, and I followed as fast as I could. A partial shoe track showed occasionally in areas that weren't overgrown with grass. I passed a half-smoked cigarette that had fallen to the ground, and paused a moment. I wanted to pick it up, but realized just in time that it might be of interest to the police. Whoever was in the woods didn't seem to want to be identified. I compressed the burning end with a small stone to put it out, left it in the mud and jogged on. Paddy was barking furiously, as if he'd cornered something. He was no longer moving away from me.

I rounded a bend and broke into the clearing where the cabin had once stood. Paddy was there, with his front feet in the water, gazing at the small island in the river. The running-shoe tracks were all over the bank here, and I also saw a straight drag mark in the sandy mud that looked as if someone had pulled a small boat up on the bank, and then hurriedly pushed off again.

"OK, you can stop now," I told Paddy. "They're gone." He directed one last resentful yelp toward the island and came to me. I patted him on the head and scratched his ears. "You tried your best, but maybe it's just as well we didn't catch him. Or her. I think we should go call Detective Milford."

We hurried home, jogging part of the way, since a look at my watch told me I'd have to hurry to catch Detective Milford at the station. Actually, I had no idea if he worked regular hours or not, but it was worth a try.

Back at the house I called the Sheriff's Office. When a woman answered, I asked for Detective Milford. She told me to hold, but I guessed she only covered the receiver since I heard a muffled shout, "Dennis, wait up, it's for you."

While I waited, I absently studied the information I'd posted beside the phone in May, when I learned I was outside the jurisdiction of Cherry Hill. The Cherry Hill Police number was easy to remember. It was just the local exchange with 4-4-5-5 (H-I-L-L) at the end. The county number wasn't memorable at all; I'd had to read it off the card.

"Milford here," came his familiar gruff voice a moment later.

"It's Ana Raven. I'm not sure if this is important or not, but someone's been out at Angelica's grave site."

"What makes you think so?"

A trace of annoyance flickered through my mind. He made it sound as if I were too stupid to know anything, but I realized he only wanted details. "I walked out there after the service today. Someone was smoking, and when I called to him, he ran off. Paddy chased whoever it was, but it looks as if he left by canoe from the spot where we found the old rowboat."

"You saw a man?"

"No, I never actually saw the person. But there are tracks all over that look like they were made by expensive running shoes. They seem large for a woman, but it could be."

"You saw the boat?"

"No, just the drag mark on the bank." I admitted. "I really didn't see much at all. It could just be someone who's curious, but I thought you should know."

"And you're correct. Did the tracks go directly to the grave?"

I felt vindicated. "Yes, there was no wandering around that I noticed. Oh, they dropped the cigarette too."

"Did you pick it up?"

"No, I thought I shouldn't touch it, but it was still burning, so I just pressed the hot end into the mud and left it in place. I didn't think we needed a forest fire. I can find it again."

"Good." He sighed. "Stay home and wait for me. I'll be there as soon as I can scare up a tech."

I made some iced tea, and sat on the terrace to await the detective's arrival, with Paddy dozing at my feet. About forty minutes later, Detective Milford and a young man I'd seen the previous weekend, but never met, stepped out of a county car. The technician was carrying a duffel bag, and was introduced to me as Cameron Slater.

"Leave the dog home," Milford ordered.

I didn't argue, but took Paddy inside and shut him in his

kennel. "Sorry, boy," I said. "The detective isn't a dog lover."

The three of us hiked back to the river once again. I pointed out the lack of unusual tracks on the path we followed, and then how they appeared and covered the bare dirt at the roped-off area. Milford grunted, and the technician went to work, pulling out equipment to take casts.

"Where's that cigarette?" Milford asked.

"This way," I said, and pointed upstream along the river bank. I found the butt with no problem. It was lying in the mud, and didn't seem to have been disturbed since I had put it out. The detective pulled out a small camera, snapped several photos, and scooped the cigarette up in an evidence bag.

"And the tracks go on farther? Your prints seem to cover some from the running shoes."

"To the old cabin site." We continued upstream and I was careful to stay behind Detective Milford, rather than chance being reprimanded for destroying any additional tracks. At the clearing, he took more pictures, long shots, and close-ups of the drag marks and jumbled footprints. He didn't speak, and I kept quiet as well, following his lead. Slater arrived in the clearing a few minutes later.

"All set?" Milford asked.

"Yes, sir. I got pictures, clear impressions, and looked around. Someone had been poking around under several trees. Leaves were disturbed, but no serious digging."

"You'll need to stay here until a deputy arrives," he told Slater.

"Yes, sir." The young man seemed as intimidated by Milford as I did, and he glanced around nervously. I suspected staying in the woods alone wasn't high on his list of favorite activities.

"Ms. Raven and I are going back to her house. You'll be relieved by a deputy who's scheduled for duty tonight. Go back to the grave." He then turned to me and pointed toward the white birch. I realized he was even more familiar with this terrain than I was. He'd probably been over it many times in the past week.

When we reached the house, he first spent some time on the car radio, while I waited on the terrace. Finally, he unfolded his meaty frame from the car and approached me.

"You did the right thing to call. We'll have someone here to watch soon. That was no casual sightseer. We haven't given out the exact location of the grave. Did you tell anyone?"

"No, of course not. You told me not to on Saturday."

"And don't be surprised to hear a motorboat. We need to check out that island."

"I'll appreciate knowing no one is hiding there."

"Why didn't you call me right away, this afternoon?"

"What? I did."

"You called me from your house."

"Where else would I call from?"

"You don't have a cell phone?"

"No, I've thought about getting one, but haven't yet."

"Do it. Tomorrow. And keep it with you. This is a murder case, and someone who knows more about it thinks you saw them."

22

I hoped the Sheriff's car in the driveway would deter anyone from coming to the house, and with a motorboat being dispatched, access from the water was being watched. I felt slightly apprehensive, but with Paddy at the foot of my bed I managed to fall asleep not long after it got dark.

Adele phoned me while I was eating breakfast. She was calling a meeting of the committee which had oversight of the Family Friends program. She said most everyone else was able to attend, even with the short notice. After I told her about the events of Wednesday evening, I assured her I'd also be at the church at ten o'clock. I asked if I could bring Paddy, and she thought that would be fine.

While I finished my coffee, I tried to focus my thoughts on the committee's tasks. With all the disturbing events of the past week, it was a challenge to think about day-to-day needs of the Leonard family. My mind kept veering off to images of DuWayne chatting with his friends rather than his family, or the deer-in-the-headlights look Sunny had developed. However, I knew we, as a group, needed to find some ways to help Len and the girls get back to normal life as quickly as possible.

Adele was waiting at the fellowship hall when I arrived. She had a large notebook open in front of her on a long table. Another woman, Geraldine Longcore, was filling a carafe from the coffeemaker at a side table. A plate of donuts, some with chocolate and some with pink icing, had been placed on the conference table already, with sugar and creamer packets. Geraldine brought over the carafe, cups, and napkins. I very much wanted to talk with the fourth member of our committee, John Aho, who had been assaulted by DuWayne's friend Larry. I hoped he'd be there, but I knew he only made it to daytime meetings when he felt things were under control at the service station.

As I was bent over looping Paddy's leash around a table leg, I saw a man's feet enter the room, but when I straightened up, it was not John, but rather the bald man Adele had been visiting with the day before. Paddy lay down quietly; he was really getting used to being good indoors.

"Everyone, meet Ralph Garis," Adele announced. "He's decided to join our committee, since he has a special interest in one of our families."

"Oh?" asked Geraldine.

"Ralph is the father of Paula Garis Wentworth. You know, she owns the restaurant where Angelica Leonard wanted a job."

Suddenly it all clicked. The large young man who had been with him yesterday was probably Frank, Paula's brother.

Geraldine got right to the point. "I haven't seen you in church lately, Ralph," she said sharply.

"We talked about that, Dini," explained Adele in a rush. Dini was Geraldine's nickname, although I suspected she didn't care for it very much. Geraldine was a large, proud woman, and the diminutive "Dini" didn't fit her. "He's on the church membership roll, and there's nothing in the by-laws requiring regular church attendance to be on a committee."

Ralph leaned forward and took a chocolate donut, while staring intently at Geraldine.

There was more tension in the room than I understood. Geraldine and Ralph apparently were acquaintances, but certainly not old friends. However, the dark mood was broken when John Aho walked through the door, whistling a lilting tune. "I think I can stay about thirty minutes, so if there's important business to conduct, maybe we could get right to it," he said. "I've got Marie watching the till, but she can't do any repairs." He was blond and bony, with a cheerful grin, and wore the dark blue uniform of an automobile service man, and it was well-spotted with grease. He chose a pink donut and filled a styrofoam cup with coffee, black. His hands were fairly clean, but the odor of industrial degreaser wafted through the room.

"Excellent!" Adele said, glad of an easy transition to

business. She wrote something in her notebook.

We jumped right into a discussion of the needs of the Leonards. Geraldine was the certified literacy tutor, and she reported meeting once with Corliss. She didn't call him Len. She indicated that he did have severe dyslexia, and rambled on a bit too long about the details of his disability, but it gave us all a chance to nibble donuts and sip our coffee. Adele asked her opinion of the likelihood of Len's success. At this, Geraldine said he was motivated, and she had high hopes if he stuck with the program. Then I was in the spotlight a bit more than I was prepared for, but I had seen much more of the family than any other committee member. I explained how close I had become to the girls because of the dog, and told some stories of our time together. When I mentioned his name, Paddy thumped his tail against the table legs.

"And Angelica's body was found on your property?" Ralph asked. This was the first time I'd been directly asked about the location.

"Not exactly. I've been told by the detective not to give out details."

"The rumor is that the dog actually found the burial site," Geraldine said. It wasn't a question, but she was clearly prying for more information.

"People will talk," I replied evasively.

"I don't understand why the body would have shown up now, if she was buried seven years ago," Ralph said, sounding belligerent. "But the paper said it was definitely murder."

"Did you see the body? Was there a gunshot wound?" added Geraldine, giving up any pretense of being subtle.

"Don't be silly, Dini," said Adele. "There was nothing left but a skeleton, according to the news."

"But a skull could still have a bullet hole in it."

I recalled overhearing Officer Brown mention knife marks on the ribs, but I didn't say anything.

"After all, how do they know it was murder?" asked Ralph. "The news article was very sketchy."

"Can we get back on track?" John put in, looking at his watch.

"Yes, indeed," added Adele. "Ana, based on your observations, do you have any suggestions of specific ways to help Len and the girls?"

"I do," I said confidently, glad to take the focus off the murder. "I've learned that the girls were raised by Becky to enjoy fresh fruits and vegetables, to eat a healthy diet. But they can't get to town to shop very often because Len finds it so difficult to drive. Their refrigerator is at least forty years old. I'm wondering if the church could buy them a new one, and make sure they get to a store once a week.

"Excellent suggestion," said Geraldine. "I make a motion we do just that."

"Second," said John.

Adele called for discussion, but there was none. She followed with, "All in favor?"

We voted, Adele wrote in her notebook again, and just that easily the Leonards had a new appliance coming their way. John said he'd check on prices at several stores, and report back.

"Remember, they live in a trailer," I noted. "It can't be a side-by-side."

One other item was on our agenda, but that service project consisted only of taking meals to a family where the mother was undergoing strong chemotherapy. Adele said the schedule was already covered for the next two weeks. We adjourned and John rushed for the door, having stayed well past his allotted half hour. I'd had no chance to talk to him at all.

Geraldine picked up her purse, put an extra donut in a napkin, and left quickly, while Adele began clearing up the trash. Ralph approached me. I already didn't care for his manner, and now he moved close to me. Either he was near-sighted, or didn't have a good sense of other people's personal space.

"I suppose you know quite a bit about what happened between Angelica and DuWayne, since you've gotten so close to the family," he said.

I took a step backwards, and he moved right into the space, again standing too near me.

"I'm not sure I do," I said. "I'm not even sure it's any of my business. I've become very fond of Star and Sunny, but I'm only interested in information about Angelica and DuWayne if it will make me more able to help the girls now."

"Frank and DuWayne were good friends in high school. We're not racist." He straightened importantly. "But DuWayne went off on the wrong track. Frank and I tried to tell him to shape up, or he'd end up in jail. Then he took up playing house with Angie, and started acting as if he were too good for us!"

Apparently, Ralph planned to fill me in whether I was interested or not. Adele closed the kitchen door behind her and interjected, "All set?"

Ralph ignored her and pointed a finger at my nose. I couldn't understand why he was being so forceful with me. "Those kids are DuWayne's blood. Be careful you don't get burned."

Now I understood. Despite his words to the contrary, Ralph was apparently more interested in warning us about involvement with the girls than in really helping them. Paddy stood and was growling softly. Adele had also heard the important parts of his monologue.

"Really, Ralph! Is that why you wanted to be on this committee? Go home and take your prejudice with you. We'll get by just fine with only four members." She grabbed him by the arm and turned toward the outer door.

Ralph glared at her and shook himself free. "I'll leave, but you mark my words, there's nothing but trouble ahead for that family, no matter what you do. Hammer Bridge Town does not spawn winners."

He stalked out the door. Adele looked at me and rolled her eyes. "I should have known," she said with a sigh. "Here, I pride myself on knowing what's going on, but I was so eager to have another warm body on the committee that I didn't catch on."

"Don't beat yourself up," I said, sympathetically.

"I'll walk you out." She picked up her notebook.

"OK." I released Paddy's leash from the table leg, and he stretched and smiled up at us. At least he was exempt from the problems of human prejudice. We exited, and Adele locked the outer door while I took Paddy to the tall grass behind the asphalt parking lot. When we converged at my car she paused.

"Did you notice Dennis Milford at the service?"

"The detective? Sure. He was keeping a close eye on everyone. I don't blame him. They say killers often show up at the funerals of their victims."

"Probably, but he was watching you a lot of the time."

"Me?" I was incredulous. "I didn't even know Angelica."

"Oh, Ana. You can be so dense. I think he likes you."

"What are you talking about? That's crazy. He treats me like a block of wood. Well, maybe as if I'm a little brighter than that, more like... a... a... cow!"

Adele was looking sly. "Of course he's acting that way. A man like that can't let on that he's impressed, and attracted to you."

This was really too brazen, even for Adele, who liked to play matchmaker. "I don't believe a word of what you are saying. I don't even want to believe it. The man has nothing on his mind but business, and he's really gruff about that."

"I'm just saying... "

"I don't want to hear any more silly ideas like this. The man was doing his job, that's all."

"Whatever you say. I need to get back to the store. Actually, I am able to stay away longer than I used to. Justin's working out so well I've made him a manager, and hired another cashier. Justin is even thinking about switching his major to business. But I hate to leave him more than a couple of hours."

"I won't keep you, then. Actually I need to go to Emily City." I really wanted to get away from Adele and her wild ideas. I opened my car door, and Paddy jumped in.

"Wait," Adele implored, sensing my desire to leave immediately. "You do need to know something, but I didn't want to tell everyone. You know how nosy people are."

I tried not to smile. Adele was nosiest of them all, but she hadn't needed to ask any prying questions at the meeting. Everyone else had done that, and she had only kept her ears open. "What's that?"

"Did you see Frank yesterday?"

"Is he the heavy man who was with Ralph?"

"That's the one." She glanced around as if suddenly worried that someone might hear, but the parking lot was empty except for the two of us. I was more worried that someone had overheard her wild speculations about Detective Milford. "Such a shame. He used to be the picture of fitness, but he came home with PTSD, and he's never been the same."

"From the Army?"

"Yes, Iraq." She shook her head sadly.

"I saw him, but I didn't meet him."

"He couldn't get away from Ralph for even a minute. But when they left, he slipped me a note." She placed a piece of paper in my hand.

I opened it and read silently, "Larry Louama was released from prison last week." I raised my eyebrows, but said nothing. I wasn't sure how this was important to me.

Adele had more to tell me. "They only sent him away for robbery and assault, but there's not much doubt that he killed J. Everett Bailey."

"Who's that?"

"He owned the Sleep Lodge in Emily City. He walked in on a drug deal going down in one of his rooms and ended up dead."

"And you think Larry did it?

"Everyone knows he did, but no one could ever prove it. He's slick as a snake."

"Why is this important to me?" I asked, doubting her accusation which she didn't back up with anything resembling a fact.

"My money's on him as Angelica's killer."

23

All of Adele's crazy ideas swirled around in my head as I drove to Emily City, but I was too annoyed to sort it all out. Paddy was getting accustomed to staying at Fur and Fins, and once again I dropped him off to play while I looked for a place to get an inexpensive cell phone. I grabbed a burger and fries at a fast-food drive-thru and cruised the small strip malls until I found a wireless phone store.

After an interminable wait with six people ahead of me, a young, acne-scarred man asked if he could help. He tried to sell me several fancy "mobile devices," as he called them, but I finally convinced him I only wanted to make an occasional phone call while away from my house. This caused him to downgrade his sales pitch to something smaller, but I was determined to buy a phone and not a portable computer. Eventually, I had my way, and left with a basic flip phone, activated for a limited number of monthly minutes at a reasonable fee.

My frustration quota for the day was about maxed out. Having Family Friends infiltrated by a racist, hearing Adele's improbable assertions, eating junk food for lunch, and being pressured to buy something I didn't want had taken a toll. To be honest, I was seething inside, and nearly forgot to pick up the dog at the pet store.

But Paddy wagged his whole body, not just his tail, when he was brought in from the play yard, as if I were his favorite person in the whole world. He thrust his nose into my hand, and when I knelt down to pet him he insisted on trying to lick my face, despite my protestations, until I was laughing out loud. Somehow he knew my efforts to push his long face away from mine were only half serious, and in a few minutes I was sitting flat on the floor, leaning against a pallet of dog food bags, with a wet face, half-crying from my released emotions and gulping with the effort to stop. The sales assistant had walked away and left me several minutes previously. Now, he returned with a woman who appeared to be a manager.

"Ma'am, is there something wrong?" she asked.

"No, no. There was, but I think it's just been fixed," I said, getting to my feet. "I'm sorry for causing a disturbance."

"No problem. Dogs can be a great comfort, can't they?" She smiled.

"They certainly can," I assured her.

Paddy woofed in subdued agreement, and we left the pet store in much better spirits.

I decided I wasn't going to let circumstances keep me from talking to John Aho any longer. With Adele claiming Larry Louama was an unpunished killer, now on the loose, I wanted to find out about his attack on John. Even though it had happened long ago, I wanted to know why John hadn't pressed charges.

Aho's Service Station was located on the south edge of Cherry Hill, and was the type of place one rarely finds any more. It had not morphed into a convenience store but really serviced cars, in addition to selling gas and oil. The parking area was small and was crammed with vehicles apparently waiting repairs. A two-bay garage beside the cashier's office was dark with the grease of several decades. The office wasn't much cleaner, but the exterior of the building had been painted white with blue trim, and someone, perhaps John's wife, Marie, had filled blue tubs with bright purple petunias beneath the windows.

I didn't see anyone, even though the doors were all open, but followed the sound of sharp blows on metal, and a bright flare of light from a drop cord. In this way, I easily located John, peering up into the undercarriage of a car which was raised on a hoist. He craned his neck toward me.

"Ana," he said. "What can I do for you?" He set a hammer down on a bench covered with grease-encrusted tools and wiped his hands on a pink rag. He quipped, "I can adjust any bolt as soon as I find the right size hammer."

His grin was infectious, and I smiled. "Do you have a

minute?" I asked. "I see you're busy. It's not about a car problem," I added.

"There are always cars to be fixed, but life's more than broken vehicles. Let's talk out here in the light." He stepped out into the sunshine, blinked and leaned his rump against the low brick ledge that created a sort of exterior chair rail around the building.

I'd been thinking about how to approach this subject, since I wasn't sure it was common knowledge that Larry Louama was out of prison. I began, "I've been trying to understand DuWayne Jefferson better. He's been upsetting Star and Sunny all week, and I can't decide if it's good or bad that he sees them."

"Bad," said John in a flat voice.

"Well, I sometimes think so too, but he is their father, and they naturally would like to have a relationship."

John shrugged.

I continued, "The person I really want to ask you about is Larry Louama. I understand that he and DuWayne were good friends."

"There's a train wreck waiting to happen."

"How's that?"

"Those two were in school together at Emily City High. Larry quit, but DuWayne finished, at least. He played football."

"Emily City? I thought the Louamas lived here in Cherry Hill."

"They do, but Larry got kicked out of school here, and his parents rented in a room with someone in Emily City, and enrolled him over there. Didn't do any good. The boy had no use for education. He quit the day he turned sixteen."

"So Larry was always in trouble?"

"Since he was in grade school. And anyone he associated with couldn't help but be involved too."

"I heard he came after you with a tire iron."

"Yup." John paused and shifted his weight. "You manage to hear a lot for a newcomer. That's pretty old news."

"I'm not trying to pry. I did start asking about Angelica, just to be able to talk to the girls without putting my foot in my mouth." I grinned. "And people tell me all kinds of things."

"That's probably true enough."

"So, do you want to tell me about it?"

"There's not much to tell. We used to have a pop machine back then, and a candy counter. Larry walked over here one evening, looking to buy a can of pop, but the machine was out of order. I think he must have been high on something because he went berserk."

"What happened, exactly?"

"I was working on some car, Jerry Caulfield's actually, as I recall."

"You remember that?" I was astonished.

"I do, but you'll know why in a minute."

"Oh, sorry. Go ahead."

"So, Larry started kicking the pop machine and cussing me out something fierce. I went out to see what was going on. There was a tire iron balanced on this ledge, right over there," he pointed to the continuation of the ridge he was leaning on, "and he grabbed it up and started swinging. Broke the front of the pop machine."

"Were you here alone?"

"Of course. Never had much use for hired help. Anyway, I reached back inside here to lay hands on something myself. I got a hold of a crowbar and we faced off. His eyes were crazy-like."

"How big is Larry?"

"Big enough. He wasn't full-grown then, but was about my size, and wiry-tough. And on drugs. At first, he decided not to take me on, but he began to smash windows and anything he could reach. I was really worried he was going to dent Caulfield's Cadillac."

"Did he?"

"Nope, I got between him and the garage door, and then he aimed for my head, but I've been around the block a time or two. Done a little martial arts in my day. He took one big swing, but I just put that crowbar in the right place and when the tire iron connected with it there was a big 'twang,' and Larry let out one huge yelp. The tire iron went flying." John had ducked his head, and now looked up at me shyly, clearly proud of a story he hadn't had a chance to tell in a long time. "And his hands stung so bad he couldn't pick up the baseball cap that had fallen off his head. He ran off and left it behind.

He was just a kid then. I probably wouldn't fare so well against him anymore."

"Did you press charges?" I asked, although I'd already been told that he hadn't.

"Now there's a funny thing. I wanted to. I called the police and filed a report right away. I sure didn't want to have the insurance turn down my claim for these big windows."

"But they wouldn't let you? That seems odd."

"It wasn't that simple. Cherry Hill called in the Sheriff's Department, and they came over with an FBI agent, of all things."

"The FBI? Why?"

"The drugs. Apparently Larry was in so deep, even at sixteen, that they were trying to use him to get to some of the big distributors."

"So they didn't want to send him to a juvenile home and lose their connections?"

"That's about the size of it. The government paid for my windows, and everything was played down."

"What became of him?"

"Nothing good. He kept on dealing drugs—everyone knew that—but he managed to balance on that line between giving the authorities enough information to keep out of jail, and continuing to make plenty of money himself. Finally ended up in state prison for cutting up someone in a fight, downstate. But he's out again, so I hear."

"I've been told that, too. I heard a rumor that connected him with the death of a businessman in Emily City."

"Yup. J. Everett Bailey. Different county, of course, but he was a bit of a celebrity. He gave lots of money to local causes. Really a big deal when it happened. He was shot in his own motel. Left on the floor, and he bled out."

"Why wasn't Larry arrested for that, if he was there?"

"I don't remember. Probably no witnesses."

"But he was with DuWayne the day Angelica disappeared?"

John nodded. "He sure managed to have an alibi on an important date."

"It sounds like they just covered each other, but why did anyone believe them?"

"That's a really good question, don't you think?"

24

Friday dawned clear and surprisingly cool for July. There were no meetings or pressing errands, and I hadn't had a chance to enjoy my new screen porch yet, so I decided this was the day. There was no furniture in the room, and the walls were only primed, but while Paddy was out on his cable run I set up the card table and a folding chair. I owned some of my family linens, and found a lovely drawn-work tablecloth my grandmother had made. With a bright-red paper napkin and a blue plate the table looked festive. I hunted through the silverware drawer to find a matching set of flatware. Then I made myself a massive vegetable omelet, a slice of toast, and a pot of coffee.

I brought Paddy in and he pushed his bony frame past me as I carried the food up the narrow stairs. The dog was so tall he could see out through the screening even sitting down. While I ate, he surveyed the trees beyond the yard. He loved the space as much as I did.

It was mid-summer, and the birds weren't singing with the enthusiasm of spring, but robins were insistently calling "cheeri-up," and various sparrows twittered. I heard a blue jay's accusing, "Thief!" After eating, I brought in a pile of pillows from my bed and sat leaning against the wall. I was too low to see anything but branches against the sky, but a light breeze made the leaves dance, and I sipped coffee and let my mind wander.

It still mystified me that DuWayne and Larry hadn't needed to do more than vouch for each other on the day Angelica had disappeared. Len had said something about them hauling sand. I supposed someone at either the pickup or delivery locations, or both, had seen them a few times. I watched the leaves and unfocused my eyes. When was Angelica actually killed? That was the real question. And it couldn't be answered. No wonder the alibis weren't important. Until this week, no one had even been sure anything had happened to her.

Finding her body made it likely she had never left the area, but unless someone confessed, it would probably never be known if she died the day she was walking to Paula's Place, or the next day, or even the next. I was no forensics expert, but I doubted the exact day of death could be determined after seven years.

And then there was Ralph Garis and his son, Frank. Why was Ralph interested enough in the discovery of the body to fight for a seat on our Family Friends Committee? Clearly, he had come to try to get information rather than to be helpful. Why had Frank given a note to Adele about Larry being free, instead of just saying it out loud? If Frank knew Adele at all, he knew that anything he passed along to her wasn't going to remain under wraps. Maybe Ralph had accused Frank of being involved with the disappearance, and Frank didn't want to discuss it with his father.

Who had been the visitor to the grave site? I couldn't figure that one out at all. If it had been a thrill-seeker, why had he or she run away? Fleeing pointed to someone with guilty knowledge, since they had gone directly to the correct location. And that could be anyone. Larry, DuWayne, Frank, even Ralph might have been there, although I couldn't see Ralph wearing running shoes. The prints were so obvious, maybe it was Ralph or someone wearing those distinctive shoes to leave a false clue. I came to the unhelpful conclusion that it could have been anyone at all. So far, there was absolutely no way to narrow the field of suspects since we had no idea who knew how to find Angelica's grave.

The sky was warming to a bright clear blue, and white clouds drifted behind the treetops. I slid down and snuggled deeper into the pillows. Adele's ridiculous idea that Dennis Milford liked me intruded on my efforts to think about Angelica. Was it possible she was right? If she was, how did I feel about it? Milford was attractive in a rough sort of way. He reminded me of George Peppard at the age when he played Banacek on television, although he didn't seem to have

Banacek's smooth way with women. I had enjoyed the reruns of that show, back when I had cable TV. I'd lived in Dead Mule Swamp for three months and hadn't even thought about hooking up my television yet, although I had brought a small set with me. I had no idea how one got reception out here; I hadn't seen a cable box along the road. I supposed I'd have to get a dish, or an antenna and converter box.

My thoughts continued to jump from one topic to another. Could Milford show Banacek's skill in solving cases, and find Angelica's killer? If Adele was right, did I want to date someone yet? That answer was a definite "no." Having one solid fact was like a corner fencepost. Maybe I could build from there.

I debated teal or plum for my accent wall. No answer for that question. I pondered whether DuWayne was harmless but insensitive or dangerous and threatening. No fence post there either.

"Let's go for a walk," I proposed to the dog.

25

My back was stiff from sitting on the floor, and the large
breakfast was sitting heavy in my stomach. Paddy whined and
lunged at a fly buzzing against the screen. Instead of worrying
about these many puzzles that I couldn't solve I decided to take
on one I could solve. I wanted to connect the railroad bridge
with the other section of South River Road, and decided if we
drove to the bridge we could find out without doing a ten-mile
hike.

My spine cracked when I stood up, and I stretched to loosen
the muscles. I wasn't twenty-five any more; that much was
certain. I carried the dishes down to the kitchen, and checked
the new cell phone that was sucking up its initial charge from a
wall outlet. Not quite ready. I didn't care. Being able to call
anyone from anywhere, or worse yet, being able to be called at
any time, didn't appeal to me very much.

When I picked up his leash, Paddy began dancing around,
and eagerly jumped into the Jeep when I said "go to the car."
Within ten minutes we were parked on the west side of the
Thorpe River beside the old Indiana & Northern Railway. I
leashed the dog to cross the bridge, and although he was again
slightly reluctant to begin, he walked the open bridge
confidently.

Once on the east side, we turned north, moving downstream
along the Thorpe. I released Paddy from the restraint of the
leash. The trail that I guessed was made by anglers to access
the bank was well defined, although in some places the ground
was low. I suspected that in the spring this wasn't a pleasant
walk. Obviously, much of the area along the river was
inundated when the water was high. Even now, there were
dark matted patches of brown muck between the trees,

although the ground right beside the river was a bit higher, and provided a dry right-of-way for the trail. Occasional wildlife paths snaked off through the woods on high ground beneath the trees. Now, in July, we had no problem getting through, and quickly came to the guardrail at the end of this section of South River Road. I debated whether I should let Paddy run free, but there couldn't be much traffic on this road, and surely I'd see any cars in time to call him to safety. I left him free.

We strolled eastward on the dirt road. Very quickly we passed the abandoned house on the south side of the road that I'd noticed when we drove this way.

"Who lived here, Paddy?" I asked. "I bet Cora knows the answer. Maybe I'll ask her. When the road still went through, they would have been neighbors to the Moshers, in my house."

This house had been painted white at one time, but most of the paint had peeled and the wood had weathered to a soft gray. It appeared to be even older than my house and had a modified Federal design, if I remembered my basic architecture, except for the ugly attached shed. I thought it looked different from when I'd seen it before, but I was approaching from the other side and the light was different. Clearly, no one had been here for ages. The weeds grew tall and were unbroken around the sad, but once proud old building.

On the opposite side of the road, the river side, an opening had formerly been cleared to the water. I thought it must have been done to provide river access to the house. A faint trail led through a swath of daisies and Queen-Anne's lace. Paddy was already poking his way along it, and I followed him. Sure enough, the river was very close, and the bank had been cut to provide a sloping access to the water. If there had been a dock it was long gone, a victim of winter freezes and spring floods. However, just downstream the river curved, and on a sandbar a great blue heron stood on one foot, alert at our appearance, but not alarmed enough to fly away. On the opposite bank, the curved branches of large white cedars dipped to the water and hid the far shore. A huge green dragonfly whined past. Until I was able to focus my eyes to the proper distance, I could have been convinced it was a low-flying helicopter. The noonday sun shone down the cut from the road and beat on my back, while the cool water freshened the air in front of me. This was a lovely spot, and I pictured residents from another century taking tea on the lawn, and small boys playing ball or romping with a dog of their own.

Suddenly, Paddy jumped in the river and paddled away from the shore. The heron flapped into the sky without a noise or a backward glance. Momentarily, my heart jumped into my throat, as I thought the current might carry the dog away, but he swam strongly back to the sloping bank and shook himself off.

"I hope you're cooler now, you rascal," I scolded. "Don't scare me like that."

The magic of the moment by the river was broken, but it was wonderful while it lasted. Paddy rolled in the weeds, filling his long coat with twigs and bits of grass. I was thankful it wasn't August when the stick-tights and burdocks would be ripe. We returned to the road, and picked up our walking pace, both needing to stretch our legs. We passed Mulberry Hill Road, and I discovered it did have a road sign; however, it was hand-painted, faded and nailed to a tree. No wonder I hadn't seen it while driving. Continuing east, we walked for about another mile and then turned around.

The mid-day sun had quieted the birds and a light breeze was keeping the mosquitoes at bay. I had slipped into a pensive mood, and Paddy was tracking something through the daisies. The road was benched here, falling off steeply on the river side, so Paddy was about five feet below the level of the road.

From out of nowhere, the sound of a vehicle, very close, bore down on me. Gravel sprayed, and I turned around just in time to see a black truck, driving much too fast for the condition of the road, heading right toward me. The road was narrow here; the driver apparently wasn't paying any attention. Not having a moment to waste, I jumped for the extreme edge of the berm. I felt a thrust of air pressure as the truck flew past me, pushing me off balance. I bounced on my rear, but momentum carried me over backward, and I bumped my head and skidded awkwardly down the gravel bank, totally out of control. The truck roared on, never slowing a bit. I ended up in the daisies at the bottom of the slope. It wasn't too hard a landing, but the fall had been a shock. Paddy ran to me and I put my arms around him and held him tight, thankful he hadn't been on the road with me.

"What was that about?" I asked him. My left elbow smarted, and when I stood up I discovered that my left ankle also hurt. I took a few tentative steps, and decided it wasn't serious, but walking home wasn't going to be a lot of fun.

Just then, I heard gravel crunching on the road again. A silvery blue Mazda crossover stopped. The bank was just a little too high for me to see who it was, but in a moment the woman in leather from Angelica's memorial service, Juanita Ybarra, was peering down at me.

"Are you hurt?" she asked. "I saw that truck swing too close to you. Oh. You're the lady I met the other day."

"I think I'm all right," I said. I stretched some more to check all my moving parts. Something warm and wet slid down my arm.

"You're bleeding," she gasped.

I rotated my left arm and saw a good sized patch of road rash between the elbow and wrist. It was oozing blood and was black with dirt. "I don't think it's serious. But, this bank is too steep for me to get back up to the road."

Once again, Paddy saw the solution first, following the bottom of the slope until it rose to return to almost road level. Juanita walked along the road and offered me a hand when she could reach me. She wasn't wearing leather today, but had on a purple tube top, tight jeans and high-heeled boots. They weren't too practical for walking on the rough dirt road, but she tried to assist me to clamber up the bank.

"Thanks," I said. "What are you doing out here? I thought you lived in Detroit?"

"I do, but I haven't left town yet. My brother has a friend who lives on Mulberry Hill. I'm meeting them there."

"Was that your brother in the truck?" I was probably glaring, but I didn't care.

"No, I don't know who that was."

I wondered if that were true. "Surely there aren't many people who drive this road," I protested.

"Beats me," Juanita said. "Look, you're really bleeding. I have some tissues in my car. Do you want me to take you home?"

I walked toward her vehicle, and was happy to discover that the ankle wasn't too painful. "My car is on the other side of the railroad bridge. Can you just take us to the end of this road?"

"Sure. Um... does the dog have to come in the car?"

"He can't really run along beside it." I thought this was obvious, but Juanita clearly wasn't a dog lover.

"He's wet and stinky. Won't he just find his own way home?"

"He might, but that's not how to treat a pet. He's not even mine. My cousin would kill me if something happened to him."

She grimaced. "All right, but put him on the floor in the back seat. Maybe you better sit back there with him. Have you got that arm covered? I don't want any blood on the seat, either."

Juanita was certainly worried about her car. If my ankle hadn't been sore, I never would have accepted a ride. However, I managed to convince Paddy to squeeze into the space behind the passenger seat, and I perched on the edge of the back seat so that my arm wouldn't touch the upholstery. We drove to the end of the road, but never saw the black truck. It must have turned up Mulberry Hill. There was nowhere else it could have gone.

"Thanks for your help," I said, as I prepared to walk down the short trail to the railroad bridge.

"No problem. Take care of that arm," Juanita said. They were kind words, but she no longer sounded interested in me. Yet, I was grateful she had stopped. I would have been really sore if I'd had to walk the extra two miles on a strained ankle, with a bleeding arm.

Paddy and I returned slowly to my Jeep and reached my house around two o'clock. There was a county car in the driveway, so I knew someone was still out in the woods, keeping watch.

I tied a zipper bag filled with ice on my ankle with a dish towel, and scrubbed my raw arm with hydrogen peroxide. This made it bleed even more, and smart like the devil. I had just enough pads and sterile gauze to wrap the forearm but would have to buy more before I could change the bandage. When I carefully peeled off my t-shirt, I discovered the left shoulder had a long jagged tear in the cloth. As the adrenaline wore off,

I realized just how sore I was.

"I'm having a hot soak," I told Paddy, as I turned on the water, and added bath salts to the old-fashioned claw-foot tub. He curled up on the bathroom rug and watched me with one eye open. I eased my aching body into the water, resting the bandaged arm on the edge to keep it dry. My eyes closed, and the next thing I knew I awoke with a jerk. The house phone was ringing.

There was no way I could reach it in time, and I let the answering machine pick up. However, as I came awake I realized I'd been dreaming of the abandoned house we'd walked past. I knew what was different today. The front door was now closed.

26

I toweled off, and slipped into yellow cotton pajamas decorated with cheerful daisies. It was only mid-afternoon, but I knew I wasn't going anywhere else for the rest of the day if I could help it. Before going downstairs, I swallowed a couple of ibuprofen, and brushed my hair. Being clean made me feel somewhat better even if my muscles were stiffening.

"Let's check the phone message," I told Paddy. I had to admit that having a dog around had given me lots of opportunities for one-sided conversations. But it was a good enough invitation for the dog and he accompanied me to the kitchen. I gave him a treat and poured myself some iced tea.

"Miss Ana." I heard Sunny's voice when I pushed the button on the answering machine. She sounded uncertain. "Could I... we come over tomorrow and sew? We wouldn't have to stay long, but maybe for a little while? Please? Well, OK... bye." I stretched my muscles and thought about it, but sewing wasn't physically demanding, so I punched in the Leonards' number. In a few minutes I had agreed to pick up the girls on Saturday morning. I would have to go out anyway, since I needed to buy more first-aid supplies to take care of my arm.

About all I did after that was fill Paddy's dog dish with kibble and fix a sandwich for myself. Then I went to bed.

The next morning, when I reached Hammer Bridge Town, Sunny and Star were waiting for me outside the trailer, so I didn't even see Len. They were alarmed when they noticed my bandaged arm. I assured them it wasn't too serious, but I needed to keep it clean until a scab formed. Not wanting to worry them, I only said that I tripped and had a nasty fall on the road. In truth, I had decided the whole thing was an accident anyway. Someone just wasn't paying attention on the narrow road.

For the sewing project, our first goal was to lay out the pattern pieces on the fabrics. There wasn't enough room on my work table, so Star vacuumed the floor. As yet, it was only plywood subflooring, but it was new enough to be very clean as long as the dog hair and loose dirt were cleaned up. When we knelt down to lay out the fabric, I learned that flexibility was not going to be my best attribute for at least one more day, but the pain was tolerable, and the girls didn't seem to notice that I was stiff.

It was a little tricky to supervise both girls' projects at the same time, but they were patient. While I worked with Star, Sunny watched and listened. I demonstrated how the arrows on the pattern indicated the direction the pieces should be laid on the fabric, and how to know when an edge should be lined up with a fold. Shortly after noon, we had both patterns pinned down. The next step was to cut the pieces out, but I suggested lunch first. The day was hot and humid, and my head was beginning to ache. I wasn't sure I was up for an afternoon of questions and chatter.

I suggested we had done enough for one day, and offered to take us all out to eat. The girls were enthusiastic since they were seldom able to do that. I asked them to play with Paddy for a few minutes while I changed the dressing on my arm, and soon we were all in the Jeep, except for Paddy. I decided he should stay home rather than wait for us in a hot car.

An idea had been brewing in my mind, and I decided I might as well see what the girls thought.

"Would you be interested in going to Paula's Place for lunch?" I asked. "We won't do it if it will upset you, but maybe it will help you remember that your mom was always looking for a way to take care of you."

"I'd like that," said Star. "It's so weird that I'm almost old enough to have that kind of job. It makes me feel really close to her."

"Is Paula a real person, or just the name of the restaurant?" Sunny asked.

"She's real," I said. I've met her."

"Was she a friend of our mom?" Sunny wound the tail of her t-shirt around her fingers.

"She's a little older than your mom, but yes, they were friends. She'd like to meet you. Actually, I think she knew you when you were babies."

"Let's do it!" Star said.

"OK with you?" I asked Sunny. She nodded, but the big smile she'd had before Angelica had been found still hadn't returned. The drive to Waabishki only took about twenty minutes on the main roads, but by the time we got there the lunch crowd was thinning and we didn't have to wait at all for a booth to open up. The girls took one side, and I sat opposite them. I noticed Madison was working again today, and she remembered me too.

"Hi there," she said cheerfully. "I see you have friends with you today."

"I do," I answered. "I think Paula would like to meet them, if she has a minute."

"I'll tell her," Madison said, leaving menus and sweating glasses of ice water on our table. The waitress sounded less surly and more professional today.

Sunny gulped some of the cold water. "This is fun," she began. "Can I order anything I want?"

"Sure."

"We sometimes get hamburgers, or maybe soft ice cream, but nothing like this." A smile teased the corners of her mouth.

"Silly, we ate out with Dad a couple of times," Star said.

"That was a long time ago. I was little and had to order off the kiddie menu. Hot dogs or grilled cheese." Sunny wrinkled her nose.

"I guess you're right," Star mused. "It was at least a couple of years ago." She sat up straight and wiggled a finger at Sunny. "You make me feel old!"

Sunny giggled and said, "You are old."

I steered the conversation back to the food. "Better look at the menu. There are sandwiches or big salads, or you can get a half sandwich with soup and French fries."

"I want something I never had before!" Sunny announced. "What's Oriental Chicken Salad? Did the chicken come from China?"

"I doubt that," I said, "but it's good. It has lots of lettuce with cold chicken, and other veggies, and mandarin oranges on top. I might have that myself."

"I want the turkey club with bacon," said Star. "And a small fruit salad."

"Can I have a Coke, too?" pleaded Sunny.

"Of course," I said.

"This is a lot of money for one meal," Star said. She looked worried.

I smiled at her. "It's a treat today. Just enjoy it."

She smiled back at me. The look in her eyes was very grown up. "Maybe I can pay you back some day," she said.

Madison took our orders, and before she was finished, Paula came and slid in beside me.

"Look at you!" She beamed at the girls. "I'm so happy to see you again, although I'm sure you don't remember me. I'm Paula Wentworth. You must be Star." She then turned to the younger girl. "And Sunny."

"Hello," the girls said, together, tentatively. Star continued, more boldly. "Miss Ana says you knew our mother. What was she like?"

"She had a difficult life, honey. That's for sure. I don't mean any disrespect to your father, but they were both so young with no real skills. She wanted to find an honest way to earn enough money to move into a real house, and buy you two some nice things."

"Were you her friend?" Sunny asked.

"She was younger than I am. Not much, but it always seems like a lot when you are in school. She would sometimes tell me that she dreamed of having a pretty flower bed, or decorating a bedroom in pink for you two. As it was, you were lucky to have a bed instead of a mattress on the floor."

Star's face was stony. "We're not stupid little kids, you know. We've heard a lot of things this week. Talk about drug dealing. Why would we have to sleep on the floor if Mom had lots of drug money?"

Paula took a breath. "OK," she said. "I'll be honest. You are old enough to hear the truth. But none of what I said was a lie. Not at all. Your mom loved you very much. I think your parents got sucked into the drug culture. Then I think Angelica woke up and tried to get DuWayne to stop the drug dealing. But once you're in that business, it's really hard to get out."

"It must be like trying to change groups at school," Star said.

"Yes, but even harder, because there's real money involved," I put in.

Paula continued, "I'm pretty sure, at some point, she stopped taking the drug money when DuWayne brought it home, and then they would fight about it."

"How do you know that?" asked Sunny.

"I do remember some arguing," Star added, looking thoughtful.

"Do you know Frank Garis?" Paula asked.

"We met him at the memorial service," Star said. "You were there, too." This was news to me, but maybe Paula had been behind me, and left quickly. I was glad to know she had made it.

"Frank's my brother. He and DuWayne were good friends back then. So I heard some things that other people might not have."

"Why would she leave us?" Sunny asked in an anguished voice, a tear suddenly rolling down her cheek.

Star looked around and then put an arm around her younger sister. "Shhh, don't cry here," she said insistently. Sunny sniffed and wiped her cheek.

"She didn't want to," Paula said. "The fact that she was killed proves it. She had no intention of leaving you, and now you know that for certain. It's really sad, but you never have to wonder how much your mom loved you. She always carried pictures of you. You looked like two little dolls!"

"Thank you," Star said. "It's nice to know that someone thought our mother was a good person."

Sunny wiped the back of her hand across the other cheek and nodded.

"Here comes your food," Paula said. "May I give you each a little hug?" She stood up. The girls slid out of the booth and let themselves be held. "I understand that you hardly know me, but if you need a friend, or some help, just call me. You've got Ana, too. You've had a rough patch, but I know you are winners, and things are going to get better."

The girls pulled away and looked at Paula. Her hug had been just right, not smothering, but just enough to show them she really cared. I felt confident that Paula was genuinely concerned for the girls, no matter what her father's attitude was.

Paula lifted Sunny's chin. "Smile?"

"OK," Sunny said, and gave her a lopsided grin.

"You can't enjoy good food when you are sad," Paula said. Madison had been waiting until the hugs were finished, but as the girls sat down again she placed the plates in front of us and then laid the check on the table beside me. Paula scooped it up and said, "This is on the house." She winked at Star, who smiled back.

The food smelled delicious. We dug in, and the taste was no disappointment either.

27

My body still ached from the tumble down the gravel embankment, but I felt as if I wasn't giving the girls enough attention, and I didn't want to take them right home after such a serious conversation. The ibuprofen had helped a lot. Much to my own surprise I heard myself say, "Since the meal was free, why don't we spend the money to go canoeing."

Both girls perked up. "I want to do that!" Sunny was now grinning for real. "Where can we go?"

"There are canoes to rent at Turtle Lake," I explained. "It can't be too much for an hour."

"What about Paddy?" Star asked.

"He'll be fine at home for that long. He'd be no use in a small boat anyway, so this is a perfect day to do it. And it's so hot; it will feel good to be on the water."

After we finished eating, we drove down Kirtland Road, and the turnoff to the boat livery was well marked. I wasn't sure how we were going to manage with three people, but the young woman, probably a college student, operating the rental booth suggested Star take a kayak, and that Sunny and I could use a canoe. "That way you can all paddle," she explained.

She looked askance at my bandaged arm.

"It's just a scrape," I assured her.

We took off our shoes, donned life jackets and with some help from the girl managed to get the boats into the water from the sandy beach without getting completely soaked.

"I'm thinking some of you are novices," she said.

I wasn't, and turned the canoe just enough so I could see the girl on the shore. However, for the sake of Star and Sunny I simply said, "That's true enough."

"It's an easy paddle to this side of the island. See the dock?"

She pointed, and I nodded. "You can disembark there for a few minutes to stretch your legs, and then paddle back. Just remember to tie up the boats, or pull them onto the beach, so they don't float off."

"We will," I said.

"I don't recommend going too far that way." Now she pointed to the north side of the island. There's a current where the river flows through the lake, and although it's not really dangerous, it's tricky unless you are experienced."

That made me think of the drag marks I'd seen on my beach, and of the dock site at the abandoned house. "Could someone paddle down the river, if they put in below the dam?" I asked.

"In theory, sure. But I don't know if there are a lot of trees fallen across the water, or what the current is like, or even what the depth is. Unless boaters keep a river open it tends to become unnavigable because of snags. Fishermen might clear it, though. Why?"

"I own some river property," I answered vaguely.

"Hurry up, I'm getting hot," Sunny said, and she splashed me with the paddle. I grinned. The fun-loving sunbeam was coming back.

We paddled out across the lake, and Star showed considerable skill at navigating the kayak. I suspected she might be a natural athlete. We easily made it to the island, and explored the shore, picking up colored stones and snail shells for a while before it was time to head back.

Despite my sore muscles, the exercise felt good, and there was a lot more splashing and laughing before we returned to the canoe livery a little less than an hour later.

The towels I now kept in the car came in handy again, and I was relieved that I could return the girls home this week without having experienced any traumatic events. Soon we were in the Jeep and headed back toward the Leonards' home.

It seemed impossible that it was only a week earlier that their mother had been found. Except for identification, the official autopsy wasn't even complete. I was sure Adele would have called me if the Sheriff's Office had released any information and discussed it over the radio. She kept a police scanner in the store office.

"This was so much fun, Miss Ana!" Sunny broke into my

thoughts.

"Why are you doing all this for us?" Star asked. "I mean, I'm having a great time, and I'm glad we're making some school clothes, but you hardly know us, really."

I looked at her, and she was giving me that same cold look she had given Paula. This week had taken a toll on both girls, but in different ways. "Hmmm. I'm not sure I can explain it completely," I began. "When I first met you, it's true I came to your house because the church assigned me to get to know you. But then we began to have fun together. That was all real. It is real."

"You aren't doing things with us because you have to?"

"Not any more," I said. "I only have a son. I never had girls to sew and cook and giggle with. You're definitely more to me than an assignment. Both of you."

"You have a son?" Sunny asked.

"I do. He's in college, almost grown up. His name is Chad."

"Does he visit you?" Star wanted to know.

"He hasn't been to this house yet. I've only lived here since spring, remember."

"Oh. I forgot that. You don't seem new. I mean, you don't act like a city person."

"Yeah, not like Dad's friends," Sunny put in. "They don't care about anything except their clothes and cars and stuff like that."

Star added, "I didn't like that brother and..."

"Hey, wasn't that Dad's truck?" Sunny interrupted with a loud voice, twisting to try to catch a better look at the black pickup that had just sped past us, going south on Kirtland.

"Can't be," said Star. "He said he was going back to Chicago, that he had to be at work today."

"It looked just the same," Sunny insisted.

"There are lots of black trucks around," I said, recalling a black truck I'd encountered all too recently.

We turned left on Sheep Ranch Road, and a few minutes later I pulled into the Leonards' long dusty driveway. Star thanked me for the day, then quickly let herself out and headed for the trailer. Sunny, who was in the other front seat, unclipped her seat belt and turned toward me.

"I don't miss her—my mom," she said. "Everybody feels

sorry for me, but I don't know how to answer their questions, because I don't really feel anything. I don't remember her at all. There isn't anything to miss."

"Maybe you don't want to let yourself feel sad," I suggested.

"Maybe, but not really. I can't miss her, because I never knew her. Grandma and Grandpa didn't want to think she had run away, so they never told us what she was like. She's like a ghost, and now the ghost can go wherever it came from and leave us alone."

"Is that what you want?" I asked.

Sunny's chin slipped down toward her chest. "I don't know. I wish she had run away, because then I could always hope she'd come back, and there would be some good reason she had to go away for a while, and then we'd be together again. Now she can't ever come back."

"I know; it's hard to have to give up that dream, isn't it?" I reached my hand over to the girl. Instead of taking my hand, Sunny leaned across the space between the seats and put her head in my lap. She began to cry. It was an awkward and uncomfortable position. I wasn't sure what would be the best thing to do. "Sit up a minute," I said gently. I kept my hand on her thin arm, hoping she'd realize I wasn't pushing her away.

She sat up, and I managed to slide over into her seat, lifting my legs over the gear console. She crawled into my lap, like a very little girl, put her arms around my neck, and leaned her head on my shoulder. The tears came then, and big racking sobs that shook her body. I just held her, patting her back and brushing the wisps of hair that had escaped her corn rows away from her face.

"I'm sorry," she said in a few minutes. "That was stupid."

"It's never stupid to be sad when you lose something that's very important to you. We all have to let that sadness out, and tears are good for that. It's what we do next that matters."

"What do you mean?" she asked.

"Some people, when they have to let go of a dream, get angry and blame everyone else or act like they were cheated. Some people get depressed and stay sad for months or even years; sometimes those people blame themselves for what happened. But healthy people kind of mentally stand up, brush the dirt off their knees, mend the hole in their jeans, and decide to find out what dream is next. People like that know they have people who love them."

"You mean, like how Grandpa and Star love me."

"That's exactly what I mean."

"And you love me too?"

"I do, Sunshine. May I call you that?"

"Sometimes."

"Just for special times?"

"I'd like that."

I pulled a couple of tissues out of the box on the floor and handed them to her. She wiped her face and blew her nose.

She giggled. "I'm really too tall to sit on your lap very well."

"Entirely too tall." I looked up into her eyes. Mine were wet, too.

Sunny wiped a drop of wetness from my cheek with her thumb. "How did you get in my seat anyway?" she asked, but with a grin. "You can't drive home from over here."

"I'll just have to push you out and walk around the car."

"I think it's time you go let Paddy out of his cage. I have to give my grandpa a hug." She gave me a quick, firm squeeze, and then showed me one of her genuine "sunny" smiles. In a flash she was out of the car, and running toward the trailer. She turned and waved to me once more from the steps. Sunny was back.

28

By the time I got to my house, I was sure my body was aching in every possible muscle, and my heart also was experiencing a little twinge or two. I let the dog out briefly, then fed him. I swallowed two ibuprofen and crawled into bed with my book. I didn't even change the bandage on my arm. I don't think I read more than two pages before I was sound asleep.

The dog was barking in the distance under a pale moon. I saw him racing toward the house with a long white bone in his mouth. There was something wrong with that. Star and Sunny were chasing after him and laughing. Paddy became the skeleton of a dog holding a fleshed-out arm torn from a body. I came awake with a jerk. It was pitch black. There was no moon and no arm, but the very real dog was having a fit. Paddy was racing back and forth between the two bedroom windows whining, barking and pawing at the window sills.

I threw off my light blanket and stepped to the window without turning on the light. I didn't want anyone who might be out there to see me. I could barely make out the dim shapes of my Jeep and the county car side by side in the driveway. Paddy was still going nuts, so I grabbed his collar and tried to calm him. Had a new guard just come on duty? But Paddy had never barked at their arrival before. I had no idea what time it was. Actually, I had no idea what time the deputies changed shifts, either. That would have been a good thing to ask of Milford, but I hadn't thought of it. My eyes were refusing to focus; I squinted at the lighted digital clock and saw 1:32.

"Shhhh, Paddy," I whispered. He stopped barking, but remained alert. "What did you see?" The old-fashioned windows were set low in the wall, so I sat on the floor with my hand on the dog's back. There was very little light outside, but I rubbed my eyes and stared at the trees where the lawn met the forest. I studied the spaces carefully, but saw nothing. Paddy gave a low growl that vibrated under my hand along his rib cage. Then I saw it. A dark figure separated itself from the trunks of the trees and moved smoothly until it disappeared behind another large bole. Paddy's growling was getting louder, but I really didn't want him to bark. I grabbed his head in my hands and looked at him. "Be quiet. Quiet!" I said softly but sternly. "We aren't going to chase after someone this time. Let's go call the police."

I hadn't gotten used to the portability of a cell phone. It was still on the charger in the kitchen, and the house phone base and handset were there too. Leaving the lights off, we went downstairs, and I dialed the number for the Sheriff's Department, again looking at the card I had posted on the wall.

"You have reached the Forest County Sheriff's Department. If this is an emergency, please hang up and dial 911, otherwise remain on the line for assistance." I had reached a recording. I chose to wait. While the call was being transferred to a human I looked out the kitchen window and once again saw a dark shadow moving between the trees. Whoever it was seemed to be moving away from the house, and toward the road.

"Officer Harvard Brown. How may I help you?"

"Harvey?" I couldn't believe my luck.

"Yes, Harvey Brown. Who is this please?"

"Ana Raven. I'm so glad I got someone I know. There's a man, I think it's a man, prowling around my house. He's just inside the line of the woods."

"Can you see him now?"

"Not right this minute, but I could just a few seconds ago. Paddy... the dog, was barking and he woke me up."

"Can you describe the person?"

"Not really, maybe a little taller than average, solid build, wearing dark clothes I think. It's hard to tell. There's almost no light outside tonight."

"Hold on, Ana."

Abruptly, I was put on hold. I took advantage of the time to make sure the doors were locked, and to look out other windows. I couldn't find the elusive figure anywhere. After what seemed like several minutes, Harvey came back on the line.

"Ana?"

"Yes, I'm still here."

"I've called the officer who is out at the grave site. He's going to try to check it out, but it could be a decoy to draw him away from there, so we have another car on the way as well. Detective Paul Peters lives in Cherry Hill, and he'll be at your place in under ten minutes. I'll stay on the line with you until one of them comes to your house."

"All right," I said. "But, do you really think that's necessary? The person doesn't seem to be approaching me. I can't find him at all now."

Harvey's voice became firm. "This is an official murder investigation. Someone has managed to keep a big secret for seven years. We don't know who it is, or the motive, or even if there are multiple people involved. We don't know very much at all, except that someone is really interested in the grave site, and your property is the easiest access. You may know something you aren't even aware of. Keeping you safe is most definitely necessary. Could you tell anything else about this person? Race? Gender?"

"Well, I guess I didn't notice a light face and hands. But that might not mean anything. The person could be wearing gloves and a mask, or even camouflage paint. I think it was a man, but I'm not even positive of that. I'm sorry."

"That's OK. It's much better for you if they keep their distance."

"I agree. I'm not really interested in being shot at." I recalled being chased through the woods just a couple of months earlier.

"Did you hear any vehicles go by this evening?"

"I went to bed very early, in the afternoon actually, so I didn't hear anything at all until the dog began barking."

"Are you sick?"

"No, I was just tired, and sore from a little fall I had on Friday." I didn't really want to explain that. "Harvey, can I ask you a question? Maybe a difficult question."

"Sure, Ana, I'm a deputy, but we know each other from church. That should count for something."

"Does Ralph Garis have a problem with African-Americans?"

There was a pause, just enough that I knew Harvey was going to choose his words carefully. "I've never had a confrontation with him, but when he does come to church, he manages to avoid talking to me, or my family. Why do you ask?"

"He seems to be antagonistic toward Family Friends helping the Leonards. I wondered if it was because the girls are bi-racial, or if he just doesn't like them because they are from Hammer Bridge Town."

"DuWayne spent a lot of time at his house when we were all kids. He never squawked about anything then."

"Maybe his attitude has something to do with Frank."

"Maybe. Frank's different now. Ralph probably wants someone to blame for that." Harvey shifted topics and became official once again. "Peters is almost at your place. He should be pulling into your driveway right now."

I heard the sound of a quiet, powerful engine. Then the night became still again. "Yes, I think he's here."

"Good. Stay in the house until he comes to you. He's going to check around outside first. I'll sign off now, if you're all right."

"That's fine, Harvey. I appreciate your concern. Thanks."

"All in a day's work. Good night."

The connection was broken. Paddy hadn't become agitated at the approach of the police car. Perhaps he'd become accustomed to the sound of their engines over the past few days. Working slowly in the dark, I made myself a cup of tea and waited, sitting at the kitchen table.

I had almost finished drinking it when there was a knock at the kitchen door. I checked to see who it was through the window, and the man on the stoop was holding a folder open, displaying a badge. I let the detective inside and turned on a light. Peters was younger than Dennis Milford. He was dressed casually, in jeans and a pale yellow shirt. His blond hair wasn't combed. I suspected he'd been called out of a warm bed to check on me. He had the good sense not to mention my daisy pajamas. I was glad the pajamas had long sleeves and covered my bandaged arm.

"I've been all around your house, and partway down the trail into the swamp. There doesn't seem to be anyone around now. No one has tried to approach the grave site either. We've kept in touch with the deputy out there."

"Thank you for looking. It wasn't really very frightening. I mean, whoever it was didn't seem to want to threaten me, but so many strange things have happened here this week, I thought I should report it."

"Exactly. Things seem calm enough. I'll leave now, but I'm going to be driving this road occasionally the rest of the night, so don't be alarmed if you hear me go by." He handed me a card. "And if you see anything else tonight, call this number directly. It's my cell. I'll be within three miles of you until daylight."

"I'm really all right. Sorry to make you come on duty." I knew that in Forest County there weren't a lot of extra law enforcement people.

"Not a problem, Ms. Raven. We'd like to solve this one soon. Old murders really rankle."

29

After the detective left, my stomach started rumbling loud enough to rival Paddy's growls. I was ravenous; I hadn't eaten since noon. There wasn't much in the refrigerator, but I opened a can of soup and made a grilled cheese sandwich, after trimming the mold off the edges of the cheese. I really needed to buy groceries. Paddy asked to go out, which gave me a moment's pause. I had told both officers that I was fine, but I hadn't been thinking about going outside myself. However, I realized if someone was still out there, Paddy would tell me about it, loudly. However, I decided not to let him loose. I clipped him on the leash and ventured only a few steps beyond the kitchen stoop. He was completely unconcerned about the woods or any noises he might be hearing. That was reassuring.

My stomach wasn't full yet, and I rummaged around and found a wrinkled apple in the bottom tub of the refrigerator. Even better, there was one square of dark chocolate wrapped in foil. It must have fallen out of the bag I'd finished off last month. I gave Paddy a couple of extra dog biscuits, then unwrapped the chocolate, closed my eyes, and let the luscious treat melt on my tongue. Amazing, how one small piece of chocolate could calm the nerves.

My arm was sticking to the bandage in a couple of spots, so I unwound the gauze and was glad to see the road rash forming dotted lines of scabs the length of my forearm. None of the wounds had been deep, but they had bled and oozed, making it too messy to leave uncovered. I'm a great believer in fresh air to promote healing, so I chose to cover only the few spots that were still open with non-stick pads and gauze. I switched to a short-sleeved t-shirt, got a clean pillowcase from the bathroom shelves, laid it across the top of my blanket, and crawled back in bed. Resting my arm on the cool, clean, smooth fabric, I opened my book.

I thought I had slept enough for the night, even though it was only three in the morning. However, after a couple of chapters, my eyelids were heavy. I turned out the light and fell asleep again.

When I awoke, it was late morning, too late to get cleaned up and make it to church. I was feeling a lot better though, and I dressed in jeans and a fresh t-shirt. The scabs on my arm were now quite dry, and I expected the two areas that were still covered wouldn't need bandages very much longer. Except that the skin felt tight, it didn't really hurt, and there was no sign of infection.

It seemed like a good day to mow the lawn and accomplish some other chores. Eating without buying food was going to be a challenge, but I wanted to support Adele and shop at Volger's Grocery, which wasn't open on Sundays. There was always peanut butter, and I still had eggs and bread. There was a jar of pickle relish and some mustard, but I'd need mayo to make egg salad. If I felt motivated, I could run over to Fairgrove Road and buy some vegetables at Bidwell's roadside stand. However, the truth was, I'd had enough adventures and people for a while, and I just wanted to spend the day alone. I almost succeeded, until Adele called.

I'd mowed the lawn and gone in the kitchen to get some iced tea when the phone rang. I thought about ignoring it, but old training made me pick it up.

"We missed you in church today," Adele began with no introduction. I didn't mind. I'd gotten used to Adele; I even liked her. She made sure she knew everything that was happening in Cherry Hill, but her heart was pure gold, and she was always ready to help people.

"I know. I overslept."

"I can understand that. I thought you might not be feeling well, or that something else might have happened out there."

I suspected Adele already knew about my shadowy visitor, so there was no point in trying to keep that a secret. "There was someone prowling around in the trees in the middle of the night, and Paul Peters came out, but the person had already left."

"Could you tell who it was?"

"Not at all. It was a really dark night."

"What did they want?"

"How should I know?" Sometimes Adele's questions were annoying.

"Well, somebody seems to be afraid of you."

"How do you figure that?"

"They ran away from you the other night, and now they're watching you. Maybe you were supposed to see the intruder last night. Maybe it's like a warning for you to stay away."

One thing Adele didn't know about was that I had been crowded off the road by a truck. I hadn't thought of that incident as part of a plan to intimidate me. But that was a ridiculous idea. How would anyone have known I was going to be walking along that back road? I hadn't even known it myself until just before I'd left the house, and I hadn't told anyone where I was going.

"Ana, are you still there?" Adele pulled me back to the conversation.

"I'm here. Sorry. Stay away from what? I don't know any more about this case than you do."

"You must," she insisted. "Actually there's one thing you don't know yet. That's why I called."

"What's that?"

"I'm so glad you told me about those footprints, otherwise I wouldn't have understood the information on the scanner. They weren't discussing details. Anyway, everyone has been working on this, Tracy and the Sheriff's Department. They even got the State crime lab involved."

"What did they do?"

"That tread pattern must have been pretty unusual."

"I thought it was. I'd never seen anything like it, but styles change all the time."

"Apparently they identified the shoe type and size on Friday morning. Those are $500 shoes!"

"Who around here buys shoes like that?"

"Exactly. They've been trying to match them ever since. They're so expensive it's unlikely someone walked around in them and then discarded them, or bought them just to make tracks as some sort of fake lead."

"Do they know whose they are? It seems as if they'd pull that person in, at least as a material witness, if they found the shoes."

"I know it! Nothing like that seems to have happened, though. But I know a few people they checked on."

"Who?"

"Frank Garis, for one."

"His name keeps coming up, doesn't it?"

"It does, and I'm not sure why, except that Ralph has been shooting his mouth off a lot. Maybe Frank and DuWayne did more than play football together, even if no one saw him hanging out with the drug crowd."

"Anybody else?"

"I think they got the Illinois State Police to look for DuWayne and check his shoes. There were conversations about Chicago, and there's no one else involved in this case who lives there."

"What did they find?"

"No matches were reported on the scanner. I'm not sure they even found DuWayne. Right now, they sound really frustrated whenever the topic comes up. They don't know who else to check, unless they start trying to match any people who happen to be Angelica's age."

"They'll never get warrants for connections that thin, will they?"

"Probably not, but I think they're getting desperate."

"What about Pablo Ybarra? His sister told me he lives in Emily City." I remembered Juanita reminding me of this when she had stopped to help me. What was she doing on that back road? I thought she had said something about Mulberry Hill, but I couldn't remember her exact words.

"I wonder if they can get a warrant on someone just for being DuWayne's friend. I haven't heard them mention Pablo. There's always Larry Louama. No one knows where he's living."

"Adele! How do you find out these things?"

"I talked with his mother in the store yesterday. He hasn't been home, but they've already been calling her because he hasn't checked in with his parole officer either. She's really tired of having her life disrupted because of the shenanigans that boy pulls. She and Marko are fine people. Larry just went off the rails somewhere."

"He's probably not anywhere around here. He knows they'd look for him near his old home."

"I hope you're right."

"Adele, I need to go. I've got to figure out something to eat."

"Is that difficult?"

"Well, I don't have much in the house. I might need to run over to Bidwell's for some veggies."

"Do you want company for a while? I could bring the food. You've got a grill don't you?"

I thought of the small tabletop one I'd purchased in May. "I have that little one I bought from you. And charcoal."

"That will be perfect. You get some coals going. Leave everything else to me."

What could I say? Adele was generous, but slightly lonely since her husband had died the previous year. I decided that spending the rest of the day with her could be fun.

"All right," I conceded with a laugh. "Come on out."

After we ate our fill of kielbasa in buns, broccoli salad, and ice cream, the rest of the day was spent in light pursuits. We chatted about things as insignificant as the colors of my walls or as important as Star and Sunny, and played "knick-knack-Paddy-WHACK" with Paddy. Adele wasn't much of a walker, but we strolled some distance out and back on my trail at a leisurely pace. The only thing that kept us in mind of the unsolved murder was the Sheriff's car parked in my driveway. The shift of watchers changed once during the afternoon. A cruiser pulled in the driveway; a deputy emerged, nodded to us and walked toward the grave site. In a few minutes, the one who had been on duty appeared, jockeyed the cars around so as not to block my access to the driveway, and drove away. We were so used to it, Paddy didn't even wake up from his nap.

30

One thing Adele and I did accomplish was to make some decisions about my painting project. We decided the screen porch should be teal and white, with bamboo flooring, and white wicker furniture, when I could afford it. That gave me something positive to work on, so first thing Monday morning I drove to Jouppi's for paint. While I was in town I stopped at Volger's for groceries, making sure I stocked up on enough food to last for at least a week.

Justin was in the office, tapping away on a computer keyboard, and Adele was working the checkout lane. When I reached her with my full cart, she said, "I've been thinking about the person who left the footprints."

"Did you figure something out?" I asked. It seemed as though we'd worried this topic like a weathered bone.

"He—I heard the prints were size twelve so let's assume it's a man—had to have known where the body was."

"Right. The police figured that out immediately. They hadn't released the location."

"So, he was involved in the death somehow."

"Yes, nothing new there."

"But what did he want? There must have been something with or near the body he was looking for," Adele insisted.

"Maybe. He'd have to believe that the police hadn't found it, whatever it was. Could there have been a clue that would incriminate him?"

"That makes some sense. But it would have to be something that wouldn't rot. Even her clothes were gone. I could see that much. So, it can't be paper or something organic."

"Could be jewelry—maybe he lost a ring while burying her."

"That's an idea."

My groceries were rung up, and I had bagged them as we talked. "I'll keep thinking about it, but I'm off to do some painting now."

"Keep in touch," Adele said. Her eyes were darkly inquisitive, like those of a predatory bird.

After one more stop, to buy cucumbers, green beans and summer squash at Bidwell's, I was glad to be done with the errands. Paddy was outside on his lead line, the food was put away, and I was ready to paint, which is how I spent the middle portion of the day.

By two-thirty I had bright teal walls and white woodwork in the porch. I could picture the finished room with the white wicker and flowered cushions, but nothing frilly. I was thinking a bold print with both teal and whatever accent color I finally chose for the main room.

Paddy had asked to come in earlier, and he had followed me around as I cleaned the brushes, and changed out of my painting clothes. He gave me his sad eye look.

"You want a walk, don't you?" I asked.

"Walk" was one of his favorite words, and he began to dance around, his long tail thumping against a chair leg.

"All right. Let's go look at that old house again. It really must have been a nice place in its heyday. I should ask Cora if the family who lived there was important. I bet they were."

Once more we drove the Jeep to the west side of the railroad bridge, and crossed the black creosoted ties that smelled of tar even after a century. When we reached the east side, I patted my jeans pocket. The new cell phone was safe in its depths, but I wasn't used to it yet, and was insecure about losing the technological gadget.

The woods along the creek were lovely and cool. Once again, I noticed the narrow trail that threaded between the trees, away from the water. I thought there must be dozens of these simple trails through the woods, made by wildlife, or local inhabitants. This one looked interesting, but I decided not to follow it today.

The section by the Thorpe River took about ten minutes to walk, and then we headed east from the dead end of the dirt road. There really wasn't any shade since sun was still high, but at least the sun was over my shoulder and not in my eyes as we walked this direction. At first, I focused on the roadside plants, enjoying the daisies and Queen Anne's lace. Occasional yellow patches of St. John's wort broke the white expanse.

As I approached the old house, but before I had decided whether I was going to just walk up to it and open the door, I saw a flicker of motion out of the corner of my eye. Just a bird—maybe nesting in the front porch, I thought. Then I saw it again. Someone was in the house. I was seeing a person in a white t-shirt passing back and forth in front of a window. I backed up a few steps, to hopefully be out of sight of that person, and thought a minute.

I clipped Paddy on the leash to keep him close. No sense letting someone see him, either. I backed up a few more steps, and cut to my right into the edge of the woods that used to border the lawn of the old house. The lawn had grown up to brush and would have been difficult to push through, but the woods were more open. There was an old fence line, and I followed it carefully, trying to be quiet. After we'd penetrated the forest by just a few yards I could see the back of the house, and it was not deserted, as I would have expected. On a cement slab, outside what was probably the kitchen door, there were several new cardboard boxes, a couple of lawn chairs, a stack of plastic bucket lids, and an ashtray overflowing with butts.

I wasn't doing anything stupid this time. I pulled out my cell phone and dialed 9-1-1.

"This is Forest County 9-1-1. What is your emergency?" came a crisp voice.

"This is Ana Raven, I'm on East South..." the connection broke. Great, maybe there wasn't enough coverage here on the State Forest side of the river. I dialed again.

"This is Forest County 9-1-1. What is your emergency?"

"Ana Raven here. Please send someone..." the phone went dead again. Still holding the dog closely—thankfully he hadn't started barking—I worked my way back toward the road. I was trying to remember the number for the Sheriff's Department, but it just wouldn't come to me. All I could think of was the Cherry Hill police number, and as I reached the road again I quickly pushed the buttons for the exchange and 4-4-5-5. I could hear the number ringing when suddenly I was encircled from behind by strong arms and both of my hands opened involuntarily. Paddy yelped and pulled loose, and the phone fell into the dirt road.

"Hey!" I yelled. "Who... Help!" The phone was still open. I struggled and tried to turn to see who had hold of me. All I could see were solid arms and hands, which were Caucasian. It wasn't DuWayne, and it wasn't Pablo. Paddy ran off a few steps and began to bark with a high, anxious voice. My twisting and kicking were succeeding in keeping the attacker somewhat off balance, but I couldn't work myself free. Whoever had hold of me was large and strong. The two remaining bandages on my arm had rubbed off and the arm was bleeding, but it didn't seem important at all. We circled in the roadway, and I saw a big foot come down firmly on my new cell phone. The man ground it against the sand and sparse gravel under his shoe, and I could only hope someone at the Cherry Hill Police Station had answered and heard me yelling before my new phone was crushed.

31

"Go to the car, Paddy!" I was trying hard to take a deep breath and make my voice as stern as possible, but my ribs were being pressed against my lungs and I couldn't speak as loudly as I wanted. The dog ran off a short way and then hesitated. He looked as if he wanted to help me, but he didn't have a vicious bone in his body, and probably thought this was some new game.

However, Paddy didn't like what he saw. He turned and walked slowly toward us, his eyes fixed on a point over my shoulder. His lip curled as if he were going to growl.

"No, Paddy. Go to the car!" Paddy circled with indecision.

The man lunged, trying to step on the end of Paddy's leash, which put him slightly off balance. I managed to dig an elbow into his ribs, and he grunted. He couldn't quite reach the dancing leash.

"Go! Go to the car!" Paddy finally got the message and began to run westward down the road as fast as he could, the leash trailing behind him. I prayed it wouldn't catch on anything.

The man now gave me his undivided attention, and I had to admit there wasn't going to be any physical contest. The man was much stronger than I. All I could hope for was to delay whatever he had in mind, in hopes that Tracy would figure out where I was and that I needed help. He began to drag me toward the house. Apparently, he wasn't going to worry about covering tracks any longer, as he pulled me through the previously unbroken weeds. I dug in my heels and tried to swing my legs from side to side to make as visible a trail as possible. I didn't waste any effort in yelling; I was pretty sure no one who might help me was close enough to hear.

When we got to the house I was physically lifted and heaved

onto the porch. The front door was opened by someone from the inside. Just for a moment I thought I might still get away, and stumbled to my right, away from the dark opening. In that moment, I saw the man who had grabbed me. He was tall and blond with bulging muscles. It was no one I knew. His bulk did not affect his speed, and with no difficulty at all he caught my arm and growled, "Not so fast, lady. You aren't going anywhere."

My logic was failing me, and I yelled, "Help! Anybody, help!"

The blond man smacked his other large hand over my mouth. "Give it up." He forced me inside the old house, and the door was slammed shut.

Despite it being bright outside, this room faced north and the interior was dim enough that my eyes needed a few minutes to adjust. Before I could see much of anything, my hands were tied behind my back with a bandana, and then some twine was produced. I was pushed into a filthy, broken, overstuffed chair. The blond man held my shoulders against the padded seat back from behind, and another man knelt in front of me and tied my ankles to the stubby legs of the chair. The position was awkward, and the twine bit into my ankles, even through my socks. When this man unbent from his task I looked into his face. It was Pablo Ybarra.

Behind him, standing and facing me were the blond man, and Pablo's sister. "Hello, Juanita," I began. "And, I'm guessing you must be Larry Louama. I've heard so much about you. It's nice to finally meet you." I couldn't believe they were too dumb to catch my sarcasm, but they didn't react to it. No one said the big man wasn't Larry, so I assumed I was right.

"Why couldn't you just mind your own business?" Juanita asked. She was no longer the polite, saleswoman who had helped me out of the ditch. She practically spat the words at me.

"You do not want to make my sister angry," Pablo said in a quiet, steely tone.

"Did you really stop to help me the other day?" I asked Juanita. "Or were you part of the plan to knock me off the road? Maybe you were supposed to find out if I'd been hurt badly enough to keep me from walking down this road. Who owns that black truck, Pablo or DuWayne?"

"You are too smart for your own good." She looked at the men, but didn't answer my questions. "What are we going to do with her? You just had to drag her in here, so now she's seen way too much."

I looked around, wondering what I was supposed to have seen, besides these three people. All I saw was a row of six five-gallon buckets lined up against one of the moldy, stained walls. My best hope was to stall for time. I turned to Larry. "I suppose this is where you've been living, since no one could find you. I guess you came in by the back door all the time. I know! That friend Juanita claimed to have on Mulberry Hill is just a good place to park, and then you can follow some forgotten trail down here without using the front at all."

Larry glanced at Juanita. "She really is mouthy. I broke her cell phone before she could get anyone, but I don't like it that the dog got away. What if he's smart enough to bring someone back? Let's shut her up and get out of here."

I wasn't sure if that meant they just planned to gag me, or if the "shutting up" was to be a more permanent kind.

Juanita nodded toward the pails.

"It will take us three trips to carry these up the hill, plus the stuff on the kitchen porch." Pablo complained. "That will take too long. Someone's bound to miss her."

"Go get the truck," Juanita said. We'll have to take a chance to get out of here quick. We can take her along and deal with her later." It looked as if Juanita was in charge here.

I no longer had any doubts about what they had in mind for me. The bandana around my wrists was wrapped tightly, but a knot in folded fabric just couldn't be pulled taut. I had been working on it with my fingers the whole time we were talking. It was now loosened, and my hands were free, but I kept them behind me. The twine around my ankles was impossible to deal with in secret, and I needed the odds to be more in my favor.

Pablo headed toward the back of the house, presumably to get the truck. Larry lifted two buckets. He started for the front door.

"Put them on the kitchen porch," Juanita ordered. "Don't advertise."

Larry changed directions and headed for the back of the house. The buckets had no lids, and as he carried them past me, I saw they contained plastic wrapped packages of something white. It looked as if the drug business was doing fine. I recalled how Juanita had described her career: "selling things to people with lots of money." In a minute, Larry was back and picked up two more of the pails. He also took those out the back door—I heard it open—and returned for the final two.

"Wait a minute." I said. "I'd really like to know what happened to Angelica, and I think you three know the answer to that question."

Larry laughed, but there was no humor in his tone. "Ask her," he said, nodding his head at Juanita, and continued to the kitchen. The outer door banged again. I was alone in the room with Juanita, who had moved close, as if to guard me. I knew I'd never have better odds, although I had no idea how I could overcome her and Larry, too.

It was difficult to come up out of the overstuffed chair quickly, but I had surprise on my side, and I lurched upward and forward, grabbing for Juanita's neck. She leaned backward, but I succeeded in knocking her off balance. She fell and hit her head on the floor, and I fell sideways against the arm of the chair. My tied legs prevented me from reaching her. I hoped she was unconscious, but the blow hadn't been hard enough, and before I could get straightened up myself, she was on her hands and knees, facing me.

As she rose, she pulled a knife from a sheath in her boot.

32

Several things happened all at once. I heard Larry call from the back porch, "What's going on in there?" and the back door banged against the wall. Juanita straightened up, and started toward me with the knife extended. Her eyes were dark pits in her face, and she pulled her lips away from her teeth.

"You nosy old bitch," she snarled.

Almost simultaneously, the front door opened, and DuWayne rushed in. I knew I was completely out of luck now. But instead of hurrying to restrain me, he tackled Juanita from behind, and threw her to the floor. She lay still; I thought she had hit her head again. The knife clattered off just out of my reach.

Larry burst into the room from the kitchen, and squared off with DuWayne. By this time, I had gotten my feet back under me, and concentrated on shuffling awkwardly, an inch at a time, in the direction of the knife, dragging the chair with me. I was too busy to watch what the men were doing, but they crashed to the floor together and the knife bounced toward me. The twine held me so tight I couldn't lean forward far enough to kneel, but after two more small steps I was able to lean over and reach the knife.

I glanced up and was glad to see that DuWayne was on top of Larry, pounding him in the face. Using the knife, I slit the twine, and freed myself from the awkward bonds.

But the men were back on their feet, circling one another. Blood ran from Larry's nose, and DuWayne was breathing heavily. "Cut him!" ordered DuWayne.

I'd never done anything that violent in my life. Although it seemed like life or death, I couldn't bring myself to stab another person.

"Do it, woman. Don't you know they'll kill you?"

Instead, I looked around for something heavy to hit Larry with. There was nothing in sight. Larry lunged at DuWayne, but the large black man jumped back. They continued to circle, like two wrestlers. I heard the crunching of tires on gravel, and my hopes soared. But the dream lasted only a moment, as Pablo burst through the door and slammed DuWayne on the side of the head with a piece of wood that looked like it had come from the broken porch railing.

DuWayne staggered, but stayed upright. However, there was no way he was going to be able to fight off the two men, and although I had the knife, I didn't know how to use it, and didn't have the courage. The only advantage was that since it was in my hands, Pablo and Larry couldn't use it on DuWayne.

DuWayne changed his tactics. "Run, Ana," he said through clenched teeth. His eyes were moving back and forth between the other two men. He was trying to play keepaway. I started backing up. With all the circling we'd done, the closest exit for me was now the front door, and I held the knife in front of me as menacingly as I could, while trying not to trip. I moved it back and forth, as I'd seen gangsters do on television. However, Larry took two steps toward me and easily grabbed my right arm, twisting it so that I dropped the knife. He wrapped me in a bear hug and held on tight. With one foot he reached out and stepped on the knife, pulling it near his body, well within reach.

Pablo swung the makeshift bat at DuWayne's head again, but DuWayne deflected the blow with his left arm. I heard a cracking sound, but I couldn't tell if it was wood or bone. It certainly wasn't going to be many more seconds before DuWayne and I would be all done. My adrenaline was pumping, but there was simply nothing I could do against the bulging muscles of the ex-con who held me.

"Hold it right there!" came a sharp command from the kitchen, and Detective Milford and Deputy Harvey Brown stepped into the room with guns pointed. Pablo froze and dropped the stick, but Larry sneered. I couldn't see his face, but I could sense the disdain.

"Forget it, old man," Larry said. "I've got this handy bitch, and I'm going out the front door, see?"

Milford nodded. It crossed my mind that if he supposedly liked me a lot this was an odd way to show it.

We began to shuffle backwards toward the front door. I wondered if Larry was going to risk picking up the knife. We took one more little step, and I felt Larry's core muscles tighten.

"That's far enough." Tracy Jarvi's official voice was more than welcome. "Just let Ana go, and step back against the wall." Larry released me and I practically leaped away from him. I spun around and saw Tracy holding her gun against Larry's ribs, and Cherry Hill's one other officer, Kyle Appledorn, backing her up.

Harvey was already putting handcuffs on Pablo. DuWayne had sat down in the chair and was holding his arm. Juanita still lay on the floor, but she was beginning to stir. She moaned. Milford fastened her hands behind her, and dragged her to the wall where she sat with her knees pulled up. She was trying to look defiant, but her head kept dropping to her knees. I thought she must be woozy. Tracy and Kyle had Larry under control, and handcuffed as well.

"I think the pails on the back porch are full of drugs," I said.

"We saw that, thanks," Milford responded. He pulled out a cell phone, and in a couple of seconds said, "We're secure here, bring in a couple of cars." His cell reception seemed fine.

DuWayne spoke up. "Juanita's the one who's handy with a knife. She's the one who killed Angelica."

"You black fool," Juanita said with a curled lip. She was holding her head up better now. "Why would I do that? Try that on Larry for size, why don't you?"

"No way," Larry said. "You aren't pinning that on me."

"Shut up, both of you," Pablo chimed in. "DuWayne's as guilty as we are. How come he's not in cuffs?"

"I will be," DuWayne said. He sounded a little sad. "I just don't want to keep hanging around with people like you. I knew you were sorting bags here."

"You ratted us out?" Larry was incredulous. He turned to Milford. "This goody two-shoes isn't innocent. Ask him where he was when Angelica died."

"They already know, Larry."

I must have involuntarily gasped. DuWayne turned to me.

"Ana, I owe you an apology. You've been very nice to Star and Sunny, but I wasn't happy about it."

"I understand," I said, but I wasn't sure I did.

"I didn't kill their mother, but I knew she was dead. I helped bury her. She wanted to stop dealing drugs, but I didn't know how we could get by without the money, so I didn't back her up."

"What happened when she disappeared?" I asked.

"Pablo and Juanita picked her up that morning. Larry and I really were doing honest work all that day. The next day, Pablo called me and told me she was dead. We all met late that night to bury her. No one had lived in your house for years, so it was an easy way to get into the swamp."

"So you were poking around there the other day?"

"That was me. I just wanted to see the place again. I've been so sorry for so long." He put his head in his hands, but winced and laid the left arm in his lap. Blood was oozing from a gash on his scalp from the blow Pablo had delivered.

Detective Milford spoke up. "It was DuWayne you spotted outside your house last night. We didn't catch him, but his lawyer called us, and told us DuWayne was keeping an eye on you because he knew Larry was out of prison, and he was afraid for you. He offered to help us catch these three, and we said we'd try to go as easy on him as possible for being an accessory to the murder. We've been looking for him all day."

"Here I am," DuWayne said, holding out his uninjured arm, as if offering it up to be handcuffed.

"And you didn't tell me?" I asked. I glared at the detective.

"No ma'am. You have quite a habit of aggressively going after solutions. We wanted DuWayne to lead us to these badasses before they knew he'd decided he wanted out of their deals."

Just then we heard more crunching of gravel and the slamming of car doors. A dog barked.

"Paddy!" I ran to the door and several more county officers were coming toward the house. The one named Chris was holding Paddy's leash, but he let the dog loose when he saw me. Paddy leaped to the porch and jumped up, planting his paws on my shoulders and pushing me flat against the house wall. He began joyfully licking my face. I should have told him to get down, but I just couldn't. I'd never been so happy to see a dog in my life.

33

The county officers took the three drug dealers away in separate cars, and DuWayne went with Detective Milford. He was being taken to the hospital in Emily City to have his arm and head checked. Forest County has no hospital. The boxes and pails were photographed, and then loaded into yet another police vehicle. I assured them that the blood on my arm was minor, just the rubbing off of a scab. Soon, there was no one in the old house but Tracy and Kyle, the dog and me. We humans sat on the edge of the front porch with our legs dangling, and Paddy curled up beside me. Most of the old railing was broken away, leaving plenty of room for us along the edge.

"Let us take you home, Ana," Tracy said.

"I'd like that," I answered with a sigh. "But my Jeep is at the other side of the railroad bridge."

"We know. We saw it there."

"How did you find me?" I asked.

"First, we got your call, but we didn't know who it was."

"I didn't know if it went through."

"It did. Almost immediately after that the 9-1-1 dispatch called us. They had heard what you said, but way too often the wireless emergency calls are dropped, out here in the State Forest."

"But I never got as far as telling them where I was," I protested.

"Sure, but they could tell which tower your cell phone was coming from. Trouble is, it's the same tower you'd hit if you called from your house."

"So you thought I was at home?"

"We did, and we went there. When we couldn't find you, we drove farther down the road, and Paddy was sitting by the

Jeep. He tried to lead us across the bridge."

"Good dog!" I said, rubbing behind his ears.

He gazed at me with his deep brown eyes, then laid his head on his paws as if to say, "No problem, I do it all the time."

"So we figured you must be over here somewhere, and this old house seemed the most likely. The worst part for Kyle and me was that we needed to drive around to another bridge to get here.

"That's really a long way!"

"I know," she continued. "We called Milford and Harvey and they got here first; they were already out of the office on another case. We all parked down the road so as not to make noise. Then we walked the rest of the way. We saw the truck outside, and then found your broken cell phone, and that made us sure this was where we'd find you."

A tow truck pulled up and began hooking up Pablo's black truck.

"How did DuWayne get here?" I asked.

"His canoe is down at the old landing."

"So he's been coming and going on the river?"

"Yup."

"I thought someone was, but I sure didn't picture him as an outdoor type."

"How's your arm?" asked Kyle. The Cherry Hill deputy was shy, happy to let Tracy do most of the talking.

"It's not bad. The scabs are mostly scraped off, but I'll clean it up when I get home."

"Should we take you to a doctor, to have it looked at?" he continued.

"No, I'm fine. I'm glad you didn't get here any later, though, or I might not be!"

Tracy was stern. "You seem to be making a habit of getting into dangerous situations, Ana."

"I certainly wasn't trying to get into this one. I called for help right away, but then Larry dragged me into the house."

"I'm glad to hear you didn't confront them on purpose. Let's get you home."

The evening was spent quietly. After a bath I examined my arm, and was happy to see that it now only needed a couple of band-aids. Every time it got skinned it looked terrible, but none of the scrapes was deep. Having a refrigerator full of groceries was wonderful, as I had choices for dinner. Paddy had earned a treat and I split the leftover kielbasa with him and made myself a big salad. The only other memorable event was that Detective Milford called and asked me to be at the Sheriff's Department at ten the next morning to give them a statement. I thought the man must work twenty-four hours a day.

Tuesday morning was again cool. I expected it to be a quick trip, so I let Paddy ride along, thinking we'd go for a walk in a county park afterward.

The County Jail and Sheriff's Department are located two miles west of Cherry Hill on the highway. I had driven past them, but had never been inside before. The buildings are low, sprawling and functional, built of concrete block.

When I went inside, I was shown into a plain room painted in two shades of gray with a metal table and chair. Detective Peters was there. He asked me to sit down and write out exactly what had happened on Monday. This took the better part of an hour. When I finished he thanked me and led me into a larger room, painted in two shades of tan, instead of the dismal gray, that was slightly more comfortable. It held a large conference table surrounded by thinly padded straight chairs. Milford was at the head of the table, and along the left side were Corliss Leonard, Star and Sunny. DuWayne sat opposite them. A gauze pad was taped on his shaved head, and he had a cast on his left arm.

There were two other men seated there as well. One was next to DuWayne, a suave black man with short graying hair, wearing a brown silk suit, and too many gold rings. Somehow I just knew he was DuWayne's lawyer. The other man was young and thin, and wore a dark suit, white shirt, and tie. It looked as if they were all waiting for me, but I couldn't imagine why.

"Come in, Ana," Detective Milford said. It was an order rather than an invitation. When I was seated, he continued. "We have just a few more things we'd like to clear up. First of all, let me explain that DuWayne has been charged as an accessory in Angelica's murder, due to his involvement in covering it up. However, his voluntary surrender and cooperation in capturing Larry Louama and the Ybarras, and breaking up the drug trade in both Forest and Sturgeon

Counties should help reduce his sentence. We think he can help us some more, today."

I looked at Star and Sunny. This must have been an awful lot for them to process on top of losing their mother. However, they seemed to be holding up all right.

Milford continued, extending a hand in the direction of the young man. "This is Special Agent Jeremy Powers of the FBI."

"FBI! What is it that you want me for?" I asked in consternation.

"How carefully did you look at the wrist band the dog brought to you, which led to finding Angelica's body."

"Not very well. It was covered with mud and dog spit, and then the girls took it. They gave it to you."

"So you didn't make any marks on it?"

"Marks?"

"Yes. Did you scratch any words or numbers on it, for example?"

"No. Why would I do that? What are you talking about? It had the factory-carved words about their shared birthday. That's all."

"Well, no, you're wrong about that." I remembered how rough the band had felt, but that was just because of the sandy mud, I thought.

I looked around at the people present. I had no idea what was going on. "Could someone explain to me what's happening here? Have I done something wrong?"

Milford nodded at Powers, and the agent took up the story. His voice was higher than I expected, but he was concise. "Larry Louama has long been suspected of many crimes which could never be proven. We think Angelica was killed because she could link him to the murder of J. Everett Bailey. What do you know about that?"

"I heard that he was killed in his motel, that's all. I still don't see how I can help. I didn't live here back then. You do know that, right?"

"Please just listen," Milford said. "The only people who handled that bracelet are in this room, plus DuWayne, who may have some prior knowledge of what we are trying to tell you."

Powers continued. "If we can show that Louama killed J.

Everett Bailey, we can also link him to several other murders in Illinois through forensic evidence from the bullets." He turned to DuWayne. "Did Angelica ever talk to you about a place where she might have kept important papers, pictures, notes? Anything like that?"

"No," DuWayne answered, shaking his head. "I'm the last person she would've told. She wanted to get out of dealing drugs. She said she didn't care if we were poor. She wanted to have an honest job, and raise the girls the way she'd been brought up. Back then, I wouldn't listen to her." He looked at Star and Sunny and rested his head in his right hand. "I'm so sorry."

Corliss moved uneasily in his chair. The girls stared at the floor, but no one was crying. There was an awkward silence.

Detective Milford's voice drilled through the pain in the room. "All right, I've asked all of you about handling the bracelet, and no one added any words, or saw anything other than..." He paused and pulled some things out of an expanding file and laid them on the table. He looked at the top paper. "...Sunny and Star - Happy Birthdays – Mommy Angel?"

I said, "No." The girls shook their heads.

"Please respond audibly," Milford said.

"No, I didn't," Star answered in an even voice. "You have to tell him you didn't, Sunny."

"I didn't do anything except hold on to it until you took it away." She glared at Milford.

"I only had it for a few seconds when you showed it to me," Len added.

"There was something scratched on the inside of the bracelet, which we found when it was thoroughly cleaned," Milford said. "Do the numbers thirteen, thirty-five, and seven mean anything to anyone?"

Practically in unison, we all said, "No."

"What if the numbers were in a series, with dashes between them, like a code?"

I could feel the blood draining from my face, and I whispered, "The tackle box under the bridge!"

34

All eyes snapped to me. It was obvious no one had expected me to have the answer. I hadn't expected it myself.

"Cora, Cora Baker Caulfield, and I were looking at some old photos. We thought we saw something hidden under Hammer Bridge, so just for fun we went looking for it. We found a small metal tackle box with a padlock on it. The kind kids use on school lockers. They have three-number combinations..."

"Is it at your house?" Powers cut in. His high voice had become almost a squeak.

"No, Cora has it. We didn't try to open it. We had no idea it had anything to do with this case."

"Can we get her here?" Powers asked of Milford, hardly taking a breath.

"May I make a suggestion?" I asked. All heads turned in my direction. "My dog, well, my cousin's dog actually, is in my car. He needs to be let out. Mr. Leonard is very uncomfortable in these chairs, and we are all hungry and thirsty. Can't this wait until after lunch? Maybe Cora would let us come to her place where there are more comfortable seats, and then we could see if these numbers open the lock on the box."

Special Agent Powers hesitated a moment and then nodded. "I presume you have some sort of restaurant in your little burg that could seat us?"

"The Pine Tree is right in town," DuWayne's lawyer said evenly. It was the first time he'd spoken. "It's quaint, but the food is good. I've tried most of the menu in the past few days."

Within fifteen minutes Cora had been called, and we were told she agreed to arrange her living room for a meeting there in an hour. She said she had the box, safe and sound.

No one had very much to say during lunch, but afterwards

Sunny came and smiled up at me. "Thanks, I was really hungry," she said.

"We all were, but I was most concerned about your Grandpa."

"I know, the policemen like to solve things, but they don't pay much attention to other people when they want something done." I thought Sunny summed it up quite well.

We made our own parade to Cora's house. I took my Jeep and the girls rode with me, because they wanted to hug and pet Paddy, who did not mind the attention one little bit. Corliss went with Detective Milford. DuWayne and his lawyer went in another car. That made me think DuWayne must already be released on bond, since he wasn't in handcuffs or in the presence of an officer. The FBI man drove his own vehicle. I knew we'd have to park along the road. There wasn't nearly enough room for everyone to get into Cora's yard.

I hadn't been allowed to speak with her, but I was hoping Cora would figure out some of what might be happening. She did not disappoint, and she must have summoned the energy of a whirlwind to prepare her living room for us. As we filed in I could see there were no boxes filled with future museum exhibits in the middle of the room. They'd been pushed back against the floral-papered walls. She'd brought in the kitchen chairs and placed them between the couch and other chairs. I knew she had a recliner, and that's why I'd suggested going to her place. It was the only kind of seating that didn't hurt Len's back.

In the middle of the room, she'd opened up one of her folding work tables, and she had laid out the photos we'd been looking at when we first noticed the box. At the far end of the white table sat the tackle box itself.

I chose one of the kitchen chairs. Paddy was welcome here, so he came in too and sat between Sunny and me. He remained alert; he seemed to understand something interesting was about to happen. We got seated and made introductions for Cora's benefit. I learned that DuWayne's lawyer was X.E. Jones, JD, of Chicago. Cora took charge. I was surprised the law officers let her, but despite her tiny frame she commanded the room like a teacher in a classroom. She explained how we had noticed the difference in the bridge photos and had gone in search of the reason why. Star was less interested in the box and more interested in the picnic photos showing her mother as a small child.

Cora's build-up was perfect. At last she handed the box to Detective Milford and said, "Based on what you told me on the phone, I believe you may be able to open this, and solve one more piece of this mystery."

I hoped she hadn't overdone it. We really had no idea what was in the box.

Milford and Powers both slipped on latex gloves, but it was the Detective who took the knob on the lock in his big fingers and rotated it. We could hear the mechanism clicking. It sounded gritty and seemed to stick a little, but the detective worked it back and forth, and finally spun the dial a few times. I think we each held our breath as he slowed the rotation and stopped at a number. I remembered it was thirteen. I tried to recall how those locks worked. You had to go back past zero to the next number, I thought. Milford moved the dial counterclockwise a whole turn. Thirty-five. Then just a short ways to the right, to seven. Click.

The room was so quiet we all heard the lock open. Milford slipped it out of the hasp, and lifted the lid. He pulled out a small brown notebook with a rubber band around it. When he tried to remove the band it broke and fell to the floor, but the book itself was in good shape. The metal box had protected it from animals and most of the effects of the weather. We could see that much, but I saw no reactions to the book. All faces were blank; all except DuWayne's. I thought I saw a flicker of recognition, but then his expression became inscrutable once more.

Milford opened the book and slowly flipped some of the pages. Then, wordlessly, he handed it to Powers.

Powers pored over the pages. A small smile began to play around the corners of his mouth. With every page he turned, his smile widened. At last he lifted his head.

"This book contains a complete diary of drug deliveries over a period of time between 1998 and 2004. Apparently, Angelica was acting as something of an accountant. There are notes of dates, places of delivery, kinds and quantities of drugs. Best of all, the person who was the courier for each delivery signed the book."

I was shocked. "Why would drug dealers do that?"

DuWayne answered the question. "We were a tight group, but Larry himself insisted on it. He was so paranoid about getting cheated by one of us that he made us sign in and out. But after Angelica wanted out, she refused to keep the book any more. I thought she gave it to Larry."

"No wonder he came back here," Milford said, sounding extremely pleased. "He needed to find this notebook."

"Bailey was killed September 12, 2003." Powers said. "Let me read that entry."

The agent flipped through a few more pages, and his smile became predatory. "Fifteen pounds marijuana, two kilos cocaine, picked up at the Sleep Lodge. The entry is signed Larry Louama. We got him."

"That's wonderful news," Cora said. "But why did you bring all these people out here on the unlikely chance you might find this evidence?"

"Because I was hoping to be able to say this." Powers lifted his head and looked at Star and Sunny. He practically squeaked, "For the person or heirs, there is a $30,000 reward for information leading to the conviction of the killer of J. Everett Bailey."

Sunny slipped from her chair and flung her arms around the big red dog by her side. I'm sure Paddy was smiling.

35

The lazy warmth of July drifted into the humid heat of August. Larry Louama was charged with the murder of J. Everett Bailey, and Juanita Ybarra for Angelica's murder. Although she kept accusing Larry and Pablo of the crime, she was the knife expert, and the autopsy had officially concluded that Angelica had most probably died from being stabbed, due to those knife marks on the ribs. Larry and Pablo were charged as accessories, and the drugs found at the old house led to still more charges.

DuWayne's case had been handled speedily, and he was already in the State Prison where he would spend the next two years. He had promised Star he'd be on his best behavior and be out in time to see her graduate from high school.

"You'd better be!" she had said. I knew she really hoped he could be there for her.

The reward money was delivered, in the form of a cashier's check, to Misses Star and Sunny Leonard. I saw the check myself, because Len asked me to go with them all to the bank to make the deposit. I had wondered which last name the girls used. Len explained that although they cared for their dad, when he and Becky had gained custody the girls chose to become Leonards.

After much discussion, Len and the girls had decided to put most of the money into savings for their college educations. A newer house was considered, but they all agreed that they didn't mind the small trailer all that much, and they'd rather be certain of being able to go to college.

They spent a little bit on themselves. Sunny picked out a new bicycle, and Star signed up for a year of tennis lessons. They whispered and giggled, and enlisted my help to take Len to Emily City one afternoon. At the furniture outlet he tried out all the recliners until he found the most comfortable one, which they bought on the spot, with a matching love seat. They were obviously delighted to use the words that sounded so sophisticated, "We'll have it delivered, please."

After that, I was informed that the next stop was the mobile phone store, where they replaced my cell phone which Larry had broken the day he had been captured.

The town was a-buzz because of the solution of these old crimes. Adele was telling everyone of her small role, and making people believe (at least she thought so) that she had done much more than spearhead literacy training and the purchase of a refrigerator. "It will do for Len for years, long after the girls are grown," Adele assured the committee members. Of course, the Family Friends voted to buy the Leonards the appliance, despite their new fortune. The money really belonged to the girls.

Len's reading lessons finally began. The old couch with a recliner section was trucked to the library. It became the first piece of furniture in an area of relaxed seating where people could read. This also made it possible for Len to take his lessons in comfort. New methods of helping dyslexics were working well, and the tutor advised us that Len was making great progress. Since he loved books so much, he was already checking out the maximum number allowed each week, and didn't seem to mind that they were books for children. "I just can't get over how I can see the words now!" he had told me, wonder in his voice.

School would be starting in just a few weeks, so Star, Sunny and I spent more than a few days struggling with the less-dangerous mysteries of fabric, pins, and the sewing machine. Oh yes, and the seam ripper. But with plenty of time to spare, the salmon top and bright skirt and vest were finished. The girls were already planning their next fabric purchases.

Finally, the day came we'd all been dreading. My second cousin, Vic, was coming to pick up Paddy. Star and Sunny had asked to be at my house for the sad event, and I had agreed that they could come. Actually, I'd had a long phone conversation with Len about this very topic. Saying goodbye to Paddy would be very emotional for all of us. And yet, I knew I couldn't keep him, even if he hadn't been Vic's dog. As much as I'd enjoyed his company, I didn't really want to have the continual responsibility for another life. I was enjoying my new freedom too much.

The girls were playing with Paddy in the yard when, much to their dismay, Vic pulled into the driveway, slightly earlier than expected. I was sitting on the terrace.

Vic stepped out of his battered Subaru, and looked around. He had returned from Egypt tan and fit. Vic is about ten years younger than I am, and he looked great in jeans and a white polo shirt. However, Paddy showed no interest in going to him, and continued to chase the ball Sunny had just thrown.

"Hey Paddy! Come." Vic called.

The dog glanced up and trotted over to Vic, but he looked at me for reassurance. Vic ruffled the long red ears.

"Come in and have some iced tea," I said. I didn't want to hurry the goodbye.

"Sure, I can do that," he said.

"Do you want to come in too?" I asked the girls.

"No, we'll play with Paddy," Star answered.

Vic and I went inside and chatted for about thirty minutes about family issues over tall glasses of tea. I had hoped Vic would be able to spend some time with Chad this summer, but I knew from a phone conversation that the timing wasn't going to work out this year. Vic's mother, Rita, was well, but Vic reported that she still thought I was crazy to live in such a small town. Finally, it was time to say goodbye.

I broke down Paddy's wire kennel and folded it. Vic carried the awkward package to the car and slid it through the hatchback. I piled on the blankets and bowls and toys.

"It's time, girls," I said solemnly.

"Don't you have to take down the cable run?" Star asked. I thought I heard her voice catch.

"I'm going to leave that up in case Paddy or another dog visits me."

"Oh, OK," Star said. "But I thought Vic lived in Chicago. That's a long way to visit very often."

Sunny was hugging Paddy and not even pretending that she wasn't crying.

"I do live in Chicago," Vic said. "But, I'm leaving soon on

another research trip, this time to Kenya. So I thought maybe Paddy would like to live in Hammer Bridge Town."

It took a minute for the girls to process what Vic meant. They both looked at me.

"But Grandpa..." Sunny began.

"Your grandpa already said it's a wonderful idea," I told them with a grin. "The things are already loaded. Shall we take Paddy to his new home now?"

"Yes!" both girls said. Sunny suddenly started hiccupping, and Paddy nuzzled her in the ribs, which changed the hiccups to uncontrolled giggling.

"You and the girls lead, I'll follow," Vic said. Sunny, Star, Paddy and I climbed into the Jeep as fast as was possible given all the hugs that were being exchanged. Even Vic was not immune from the happy embraces.

The dog and both girls were in the back seat of the Jeep bouncing with joy. Vic came over to shut the back door and fondled the dog's red head. He asked playfully, "Hey Paddy, weren't you bored in this old dead swamp all summer? It looks like nothing much ever happens here."

Notes and Acknowledgements

Special acknowledgement is due to Farah Evers, of faraheversdesigns.com, who designed the cover for this book, and then allowed me to complete the back cover to match the other volumes. I highly recommend her work.

The Mason County Sheriff's Office answered questions about drugs, hopefully preventing any serious mistakes in the pertinent chapters.

I would also like to thank my volunteer beta readers: Ellen Lightle, Barry Matthews, and Martyn Halm. No author can catch all mistakes, and I know this book has been improved by their input. After all is said and done, I take responsibility for any errors.

PUBLISHED WORKS BY
JOAN H. YOUNG

Non-Fiction:

North Country Cache: Adventures on a National Scenic Trail Trail (2005 Independent Publishers, third place IPPY award, Regional non-fiction)

Would You Dare?

Devotions for Hikers

Get Off the Couch with Joan

Fall Off the Couch Laughing

Fiction:

News from Dead Mule Swamp

The Hollow Tree at Dead Mule Swamp

Paddy Plays in Dead Mule Swamp

Bury the Hatchet in Dead Mule Swamp

Toby and Harry (short story)

Now Then When (poem in the anthology Elements of Life)

ABOUT THE AUTHOR

Joan H. Young has enjoyed the out-of-doors her entire life. Highlights of her outdoor adventures include Girl Scouting, which provided yearly training in camp skills, the opportunity to engage in a ten-day canoe trip, and numerous short backpacking excursions. She was selected to attend the 1965 Senior Scout Roundup in Coeur d'Alene, Idaho, an international event to which 10,000 girls were invited. She has ridden a bicycle from the Pacific to the Atlantic Ocean in 1986, and on August 3, 2010 became the first woman to complete the North Country National Scenic Trail on foot. Her mileage totaled 4395 miles. She often writes and gives media programs about her outdoor experiences.

In 2010 she began writing more fiction, including several award-winning short stories with Twin Trinity Media. *Paddy Plays in Dead Mule Swamp* is the third story in the Anastasia Raven mystery series.

Visit booksleavingfootprints.com for more information.

Made in the USA
Columbia, SC
18 May 2021